D0700494

To the Manor Dead

A JANET'S PLANET MYSTERY

To the Manor

SEBASTIAN STUART

Dead

MIDNIGHT INK
WOODBURY, MINNESOTA

To the Manor Dead: A Janet's Planet Mystery © 2010 by Sebastian Stuart. All rights reserved. No part of this book may be used or reproduced in any manner whatsoever, including Internet usage, without written permission from Midnight Ink, except in the case of brief quotations embodied in critical articles and reviews.

First Edition
First Printing, 2010

Book design and format by Donna Burch
Cover design by Lisa Novak
Cover illustration © Glenn Gustafson
Editing by Connie Hill

Midnight Ink, an imprint of Llewellyn Worldwide Ltd.

Library of Congress Cataloging-in-Publication Data

Stuart, Sebastian.
  To the manor dead : a Janet's planet mystery / by Sebastian Stuart. — 1st ed.
      p.   cm. — (Janet's planet)
Summary: "After a disastrous marriage and a crippling case of career burnout, Janet Petrocelli—fit, forty(ish) and fed up—closes her New York City psychotherapy practice and moves to the Hudson Valley. She buys a building in an old river town, opens a 'junque' store, and moves into the apartment upstairs. A calmer life would be nice, with a little less input from 'that overrated, self-obsessed, narcissistic species—the human race.'"—Provided by publisher.
  ISBN 978-0-7387-2293-1
  I. Title.
  PS3569.T827T6 2010
  813'54—dc22   2010017439

This is a work of fiction. Names, characters, places, and incidents are either the product of the author's imagination or are used fictitiously, and any resemblance to actual persons, living or dead, business establishments, events, or locales is entirely coincidental.

Midnight Ink
Llewellyn Worldwide Ltd.
2143 Wooddale Drive
Woodbury, MN 55125-2989
www.midnightinkbooks.com

Printed in the United States of America

DEDICATION

For
Chris Tanner,
tried and true
(and so much fun)

ONE

It was raining, pouring, cascading down the front window in gray sheets—cats and dogs *and* lions and tigers and bears. Fine with me. Less chance that some member of that overrated, self-obsessed, narcissistic species—the human race—would darken my shop door. I could hang out with Sputnik, Lois, and Bub, get a few lamps rewired, frame a picture, wax a table, and get going on hiring someone to help out on weekends, when the place actually pulled in a few customers.

I made myself a pot of coffee. Out of a *can*, thank you—this whole mocha-latte-Sumatra-chino thing bugs me. Does *everything* have to have five-dozen goddamn *pucci-gucci* variations? If you ask this gal, too many choices equal one thing: a tension headache.

While it was brewing I made up a small sign reading "Part-Time Help Wanted—Weekends." I put it in the front window, slipped in a CD—French cocktail pop—filled my mug, and headed to my workshop, a big room at the back of the store. Sputnik followed me on foot, Bub flew down and hitched a ride on his

1

rump, and Lois just lay there curled on her favorite spot, a ratty old armchair with great bones that I would have loved to get rid of, but was afraid to sell. I've seen too many psychotic cats in my day. And psychotic people.

I've seen *way* too many psychotic people.

TWO

JUST AS I WAS about to start cutting a mat for a circa-1920 photograph of a bearded circus lady playing hopscotch, the bell jangled out in the shop. What fresh hell is this? I went out front to find an enormous umbrella—a fancy-ass one, all floral, one spoke bent—facing me across the store. The umbrella closed halfway, then jerked back open; this happened several times, accompanied by murmurs of frustration.

I crossed the store. "Need a hand?"

The umbrella moved down, revealing a woman I pegged on the far shore of seventy. She looked at me and, like a switch, her face softened, got all dreamy and ethereal, like she was channeling Blanche Dubois. "Why, aren't you kind," she said in this upper-crusty voice. She had good bones and pale blue eyes, had probably been a beauty once, but she'd hit a few landmines on her detours and had ended up with a haunted, ravaged look. I got a whiff of expensive perfume, but it smelled a little stale.

I took the umbrella from her and wrestled it closed.

She looked around the store, filled with the outflow of my twenty-five years of obsessive-compulsive collecting. She looked sort of taken aback, but said, "What a charming shop."

"Thanks." Even though 75 percent of my stuff was borderline junk, I hoped the place had a certain funky charm. I got a lot of help putting it together from my pal George, who lived down the street and had that gay-gene thing happening.

"Is there any leeway in your no-smoking policy?" she asked.

"Go ahead," I shrugged.

She took out a pack of convenience-store generics and lit up, sighing with relief on the first puff. She was gaunt-skinny, wearing a long, belted raincoat—dingy, the belt was frayed—and scuffed-up black flats that were soaked; her hair was hidden under a silk scarf that sort of matched the fancy umbrella. Her beauty was a memory, but it lived on in the tilt of her chin—slightly upward, as if to show off her best angle—and the way she handled her cigarette, like she was in a ballet or something. The bitten nails were a classy touch.

"May I sit down?" she asked.

"Sure," I said, gesturing to a 1950s sofa upholstered in a black-and-pink boomerang print. It was a flea-market find I'd put out the week before, sure it would get snatched up by one of the downtown hipster-artsy types who, in the years after 9/11, had bought up every shack here in the Hudson Valley and up in the Catskills.

She sat, pulled off her scarf, and shook her head like she was in a shampoo commercial—too bad her pale hair was thin, brittle, and stuck out like loose straw from a bale. She crossed her legs, took a deep pull of her cigarette, lowered her voice, and said, "I have something that might interest you." Then she looked out the window at the rain—was that fear in her face?

"I'm listening."

She looked at me with watery, beseeching eyes. "I'm terribly thirsty."

"Would you like a glass of water?" Her look stayed the same. "How about a glass of wine?"

She smiled. "How thoughtful."

Hey, it *was* eleven in the morning.

"Some weather," I said, heading over to the half fridge. "I've got a bottle of white open."

"Sounds enchanting."

I didn't tell her it was *Chateau Plastique*, pulled from the two-dollar bin at the Liquor Locker. I filled a New Orleans souvenir glass half full and handed it to her.

"Thank you," she said, taking a long sip, smiling. "I love the rain. It feels safe, as if one can hide."

You didn't need my psych degree to know that something had gone south big-time in this gal's life. I felt my old curiosity itch flare up—I wanted to know *everything* about her.

Cool it, Janet, you're an antiques-collectibles-whatever dealer now. Not a psychotherapist. You closed your practice in the city and moved the hell up here to get away from other people's problems, and as soon as one lost soul walks in the door, you're hooked. You owe this lady nothing. Nada. Zip. You owe yourself a life.

"So, I'm guessing you have some stuff you want to sell," I said, walking back to my desk and sitting behind it, like the professional I was pretending to be.

"I do, yes." She took another long sip of wine and settled into the sofa. Her eyes were getting glassy, her smile wistful. Classic fallen-angel drunk: soulful, sensitive, mucho screwed-up. Just the type that could suck me in like a vacuum cleaner if I let them. "By the way, my name is Daphne … Daphne Livingston."

"Nice to meet you. I'm Janet Petrocelli."

"Ah, Italian."

"Half."

"Trieste is magical."

"Never been."

"Oh, but you must go."

"It's on my list. Now what's on yours?"

"Well, I have some … *things* … I would like to sell. Some of them rather … *quickly*, if possible." She clutched the collar of her coat around her neck. "I want to get away … for a while."

"Are we talking furniture, art, rugs?"

"A little of everything. Well, actually, quite *a lot* of everything. I've brought a few photos. I thought that might well help."

"It might well."

She looked at me, and then down at her empty glass. I walked over and refilled it. She took a sip, opened her purse—black leather, scuffed up—and took out an envelope. "Here you are."

I sat back at my desk and took out the pictures, fanned through shots of Oriental rugs, graceful old chairs and tables—the kind with inlay and carvings—oil portraits and landscapes in heavy frames. This was serious stuff. It wasn't for me, way too much money, not to mention expertise. I was a bottom feeder—a flea market, yard sale, and junk shop junkie doing her bit for recycling.

The phone rang.

6

"Janet's Planet."

"Good morning, starshine."

It was Zack, no surprise. My boyfriend/whatever of five months, a laid-back landscape "architect" who operated on Rip Van Winkle time. Zack had come into the shop one day claiming to be looking for garden furniture. What he was really looking for was to get laid. Well, he did. Guess what—so did I. A gal's got needs. Zack could be fun, he could be annoying, but he was easy and hunky and support-ive—and he was definitely *not* get-serious-with material. Thank God. After two dismal marriages, getting serious was the last thing I wanted.

"What's up, Zack?"

"I am—wish you were here to help me out with it."

"Okay, I'm going to hang up now."

He laughed. "Oh, come on, baby, I can't work in this rain, you won't have any customers, why not close up the shop and come on out here, we can be little snuggle bunnies, just spend all day in bed listening to the rain on the roof."

"Actually, I've got a customer here right now."

"Oh."

"We'll talk."

"Have a snuggle-bunny day."

"Yuk." I hung up and went back to Daphne's photographs. "I think you came to the wrong place. I'd advise you to take these pictures over to one of the high-end shops in Hudson."

"Oh, I couldn't possibly do that. You see, I live over on that side of the river." That didn't surprise me—the east side of the Hudson was fancy-pants central. "I have to be … discreet. I'm sure you can understand."

"I'm sure I can. But I think you're out of my league."

I stuffed the pictures back in the envelope.

"Janet, I find you … *sympathique*. Your face, your eyes. And I love your taste in music. It takes me back to St. Germain—long gray afternoons filled with wine, men, and … longing." She did that Blanche Dubois thing again, eyes unfocused, all dreamy. Then she looked at me and smiled; there was kindness in her eyes, spiked with resignation and sadness. "I know that some of my possessions are quite valuable. But I'm looking to establish a *relationship* with someone who can help me sell them. Someone like you."

"Why me?"

"Because I can tell you're trustworthy. And could probably use the business. I stopped in at that charming little *boite* across the street for a piece of lemon meringue pie. It's the *only* thing I'll eat for breakfast. I asked the owner if she might know someone who would be interested in buying a few things. She steered me to you."

That's Abba—meet a freak, send her to Janet. Actually I owed her thanks—I did some quick calculating and realized I could keep myself fed and clothed for a decade just acting as a middleman for Daphne's stuff. Do a little research, take the pictures to a high-end dealer down in the city or over in Hudson, make sure she got a fair price. I could handle that. Probably.

"Listen, maybe we can do some business together. Why don't we start slow? Maybe with one or two pieces?"

"That sounds wonderful." She looked down at her hands. When she looked up, there was that hint of fear in her eyes. "I would like to begin as soon as possible."

"Name your time."

"Can you come over to my house tomorrow?"

"Sure."

Lois got down from her armchair, walked over to the sofa, leapt up, and rubbed herself against Daphne. This was rare. Lois appeared on my fire escape one day—filthy, with half her left ear missing—to claim me as her slave. She deigned to accept my food and shelter, and let me scoop up her shit, but made damn sure I didn't expect anything—like, say, a little gratitude or affection—in return. She had less truck with the human race than I did. So I took her cozying up to Daphne as a sign that she was one of us, the sisterhood of wounded chicks.

Daphne petted Lois and when she looked up at me those pale blue eyes were filled with tears. "I've made a terrible mess of my life."

My first instinct was to say "Tell me all about it." But those days were over o-v-e-r *over*. I took a sip of coffee and said, "You've got a lot of company." We just sat there for a minute, with the jazzy, melancholy French music as accompaniment.

"It's my own fault," she said, still petting Lois. "When you're young you think you can just shrug off your mistakes—*la-di-da*—but you can't. They stay with you. Always."

Didn't I know it? And I didn't just learn it from the parade of messed-up, whacked-out, screw-loose clients I'd seen during the fifteen years I hung out my shingle. Me and mistakes had been acquainted for a long time. And I had the scars to prove it. There were the two marriages, the second of which had curdled like rancid milk just before I moved up here. It feels pretty lousy when you misjudge someone as totally as I did, when you think a person is solid and honest and cares about you, and then he turns out to be a dipshit fuckwad from hell. Not that I have any residual anger toward the Asshole. But that wasn't even my worst wound—nope, numero uno was still fresh after twenty-five years, still too fresh, in fact, to talk about.

Our fuck-ups and losses, the big ones, become part of our psychological DNA, integrated into our emotional wiring. That's what bugs me so goddamn much about the psycho-pop gospel of "get over your pain"—like tsunami-sized sadness and grief and regret were pesky little pebbles in your shoe that you could just shake out and keep on trucking. Bullshit. The trick is to take it from acute agony to it's-not-fucking-up-my-head-and-making-me-act-like-a-needy-dweeb-on-a-daily-basis. It was my credo with my clients: let's talk about your traumas, understand them, make some kind of peace, and then move forward *with* them. 'Cause, baby, those suckers ain't going nowhere.

"It's been men," Daphne said. "I was born into great privilege, but under the privilege there were a lot of secrets and ... ugliness. I fled. Into the arms of men. You see, I wanted the stars *and* the moon, too. Well, I almost got them ..." She let out a rueful laugh.

"Yeah?"

Cool it, Janet, no way are you going to be Daphne's shoulder, especially not at these rates.

"So, about tomorrow," I said firmly.

She polished off her wine and put out her cigarette in a cool Deco standing ashtray that I was having a hard time selling. Nobody smoked anymore, and those who did kept quiet about it. I figured my best shot was some rich Woodstock pothead.

Daphne stood up and put her scarf back on, tying it under her chin like she was Audrey Hepburn or something. "My address is

Westward Farm, on River Road in Rhinebeck, about a mile north of the bridge. Come in the late morning, around this time. It's the main house, at the end of the drive. I'm on the *left* side of the house. Just come in, the door is always unlocked. I'll be upstairs, in my bedroom. You'll find me. It's been such a pleasure, Janet. I look forward to our partnership."

Then she stepped out into the monsoon. She opened her umbrella and it immediately got whipped inside out. She gasped and let it go, it skittered away. I grabbed an umbrella and went out. I opened it and held it over her. She looked at me as if I had just saved her life.

"Where's your car?"

She pointed up the street, to an old Mercedes. She slipped her arm through mine and I escorted her to her car, and around to the driver's side. She opened her purse to get her keys, then stopped. She looked at me, took my free hand, and held it to her cheek for a moment.

Then she got in her car and drove off.

THREE

"Janet!" I looked across the street—George was poking his head out of Chow, Abba's restaurant. "Come here!"

"My shop's unlocked!"

"In this weather, baby, the worst that could happen is a fish swimming in!"

I crossed the street and followed George inside. Chow was an old luncheonette and Abba had pretty much left it "as is" since she'd bought it five years ago. The place was between breakfast and lunch, but there were still customers. Abba pulled them in no matter what the weather. It was partly her chill-pill atmosphere, but it was also her cooking—a pungent, fearless fusion that reflected her years of traveling the world with fifty bucks and a backpack. Her talent had earned her a growing reputation and she ran a small catering business on the side. There were about a dozen characters hanging out, the kind of people who have no place to go and all day to get there—over-the-hill hippies, artists real or imagined, folks who got out of the frenzy with *just enough* dough, boozers and reefer-heads, retirees, lowlife skanks living just this side of legal.

"Let's have a cuppa joe," George said, and I could tell from his tone that something was up. He was wearing a FUR IS DEAD T-shirt, a beret set at a jaunty angle, baggy harem pants, some very cool Nikes, and a little bling on his fingers and around his neck. Dude hated attention. George was an emergency room nurse who'd been smart enough to buy a couple of buildings in town years ago. He had eight apartments and two storefronts earning him a tidy income, and these days he only worked when he wanted to. He was pulling forty, bald, chunky, yet somehow handsome, with enormous eyes behind cool angular glasses. Resourceful, tough, and passionate, George had taken me under his wing when I first moved up here and given me endless advice on how to make my shop click. Or at least not clunk.

Abba's waitress, Pearl—who had come with the place—brought us two cups of coffee. Pearl was a slow-moving seventy-something with gray hair, gray eyes, gray teeth, and gray skin. No matter what was happening, or how busy the place was, she wore the same vacant, dazed expression—the earth could split open under her feet and it wouldn't register. As George put it: "Her elevator doesn't go to the top floor."

"Listen, babe, I'm counting on you for Thursday's town meeting," George said.

George was rabid about saving the Hudson Valley from the greedbag developers who wanted to line the riverbank with high-rise condos. Vince Hammer, a Trump wannabe with deep pockets and political pull, was trying to put up a mini-city on eighty acres of Sawyerville riverfront. It would bring in sickening amounts of traffic, raise taxes, obliterate the views, overload the infrastructure, and fuck up the character of the town.

Hammer had made his money down in the city and decided a few years back that the Hudson Valley was the next hot place. He'd built a mountaintop mansion outside of Woodstock and was spending a lot of time locally, throwing his cheesy, gold-plated weight around. George was in the thick of the fight to stop him.

"I'll be there," I said.

Just then the lights went out, the place went dim in the reflected rain. Abba came out of the kitchen carrying a cake that had a single candle burning on top.

"Happy anniversary to you," she sang—to me.

George picked up the song, then some of the customers piped in.

"Happy anniversary, dear Janet. Happy anniversary to you!"

I grudgingly blew out the candle, everyone applauded, and the lights went on.

"What the hell was that about?" I said.

"It's your one-year anniversary in Sawyerville," Abba said.

So it had been a year since I'd closed my practice and left Brooklyn—overwhelmed by my clients' endless outpouring of heartache and anxiety, my own regret and rage over marrying the Asshole, that long-ago decision that continued to haunt me, and just the whole goddamn jingle-jangle, global-frying, info-wired *mishigas* of twenty-first century life—and taken my savings, gathered my accumulated *junque* from the three storage spaces I rented, bought the small brick building that housed my store down and my apartment up, and begun my new life in a river town where I didn't know a soul.

Big f'ing deal.

"This cake is new—pecan-coconut-blackberry," Abba announced to the house. Everyone morphed into eager little guinea pigs—a new cake from Abba really was a big f'ing deal.

As the cake was cut, George leaned into me, "So, Abba tells me you got a visit from Lady Livingston this morning."

"You know her?"

"Only by reputation."

I took a bite of cake—frosted nirvana, moist to the point of melting, the blackberries a just-tart-enough counterpoint to the rich pecans and coconut. The whole joint was quiet in communal bliss.

"Abba, this cake is *amazing*," George moaned. He was very in touch with his senses. All of them.

"Not bad," Abba said. "I better try and get it down before I forget it. Come on back."

George and I followed her into the kitchen and sat on stools while she made notes on a file card. Abba never used cookbooks—"that's copying, not cooking"—so when she had a hit, she rushed to write it down. As she was scribbling, she asked, "So, how did it go with Daphne Livingston?"

"She wants to sell some stuff. What's her story?"

Abba knew all the legend, lore, and lunacy of the Hudson Valley—her clan had been here for a long time. Her great-great granddad worked on the pleasure boats that carried people up the river, out of the city's heat, in the nineteenth century. The boats docked in the village of Catskill; from there folks would take the railroad up into the cool mountain air. Abba's ancestor settled in Catskill with his wife, one of the first black families. And even though

Abba, who was now in her mid-forties, had been just about everywhere and done just about everything, she ended up back in the valley. She was tall and strong and beefy, with a wide-open face, a gap-toothed smile, and enormous green-brown eyes. She leaned against the counter and took a sip of coffee.

"Well, the Livingstons used to *own* a big chunk of the Hudson Valley. They got one of the original land grants from the King of England," she said. "But like a lot of the valley's old grandee clans, there's been a certain, shall we say, *deterioration* over the generations. Daphne Livingston has lived a life and a half. She was a major beauty, the debutante *du jour*, dated movie stars and royalty, a Kennedy or two. She painted and wrote poetry, had a few art shows, published a book of poems, was in the thick of the whole society-literary scene down in the city. She was at Capote's Black and White Ball. Then she moved to London, ran with the Stones, the Beatles, that whole crowd, even acted in a couple of European movies. But she had a few little self-destructive traits, like gin and drugs and nasty men. Then she disappeared, turned up in Morocco years later. From what I've heard she got involved with some *very* nefarious characters down there, we're talking prostitution, smuggling."

Pearl shuffled into the kitchen and handed Abba an order. She moved to the stove, cracked a couple of eggs into a pan, tossed in some fresh herbs, a dollop of mustard, and began to scramble. "Five years ago Eugenia Livingston, the matriarch of the clan, kicked the bucket at age ninety-seven. She was a world-class snob and a world-class bitch, very competitive with her daughter. With her gone, Daphne finally came home to Westward Farm. She was burnt-out and broke, and she's pretty much been a recluse over in that mansion of hers—I should say hers and her brother's. Who *hate* each other. Which is why the place is split in half—right down the middle. Even so, carrying half a spread like that one ain't cheap. I'd say Daphne is probably hanging on by her fingernails. That's why she came knocking at your door this a.m."

Abba slid the eggs onto a plate, added home fries, avocado slices, a hunk of cornbread, and put the plate on the pass-through. "Order up."

"She was scared of something," I said.

"Maybe her past is coming back to pay a little uninvited visit," Abba said. "The past has a way of doing that."

"I'm reminded of that every time my herpes breaks out," George cracked. "But this Livingston saga sounds juicy. Are you going over there?"

"Tomorrow morning," I said.

"Want some company?"

"I think my first visit should be solo. So, Abba, the house is divided in two?"

"Yes. Things got very ugly when old lady Livingston kicked. Daphne and Godfrey, that's her brother, got into a battle royal. The Livingstons are what you call land poor, but we all know what six hundred acres and an old mansion on the Hudson are worth. There was a lot of nasty publicity, charges of alcoholism, incest, insanity, you name it. There were even whispers that old Mrs. Livingston didn't die of natural causes."

"You mean...?" George said.

"Yes, somebody helped her along. Of course, at ninety-seven it's hard to tell. But the old gal had the last laugh, her will granted both Daphne and Godfrey lifetime tenancy in the house, and put a conservation easement on the estate so it can never be broken up and turned into Hideous on the Hill."

"Kick ass, Eugenia!" George said.

"The bottom line is they both have equal claim on Westward Farm, and so they just put up a wall dead center in the house. She stays on her side, he on his."

"What's he like?" I asked.

"I've never clapped eyes on him. He's reclusive, too, and apparently *very* eccentric. I understand his household is pretty bizarre. He's a little younger than Daphne."

"Tomorrow should be interesting, but right now I better get back to my shop," I said. "And please—no more damn cakes."

FOUR

THE RAIN WAS STILL coming down hard. I dashed across the street—a teenage girl was huddled in the shop doorway, her face almost hidden under the hood of her pink plastic raincoat.

She pointed to the Help Wanted sign I had stuck in the window.

"Come on in."

She followed me into the store and the first thing I noticed was her limp—one leg was a little shorter than the other. The cheap rain slicker was several sizes too small; her bony wrists stuck out and made her look like she was about eight years old. She had dark hair, a closed wary face, and stooped, guarded body language. She looked about as right for retail as I was for the NFL.

"I'm Janet," I said, sitting behind my desk. "Have a seat."

She perched on the edge of a straight-backed chair.

"I'm ... Josie." Her voice was halting, almost apologetic; she didn't meet my eye.

"No last name?"

She hesitated, before mumbling, "Alvarez."

"All right, Josie Alvarez, tell me a little about yourself."

She noticed Bub, sitting on his swinging perch. Her eyes lit up for a second, just a second.

"I need a job."

"That's it?"

She nodded.

"Well, why do you think this would be a good job for you?"

"Because it pays money."

"That's an honest answer."

"I am honest. Dependable."

"Are you from Sawyerville?"

Josie nodded.

"You in high school?"

She shook her head.

"You finished?"

"I dropped out."

"You live with your family?"

Her mouth tightened, she looked down, took a shallow breath, nodded.

"Tell me more: Mom, Dad, brothers, sisters?"

"My mother and her boyfriend and their baby."

I knew this story: Josie was the odd one out, the Mom's older kid who had no place in the new family. But there was more here, something darker. And where did the limp come from?

"You know anything about old stuff?"

Josie shook her head.

She looked me in the eye for the first time—I saw a little kid adrift in a big sea.

All right, Janet, end the interview, send her on her way. She's in big trouble, something nasty is happening at home, she needs so much more than a job, so much more than you could possibly give her. The last thing your shop—or your life—needs is some messed-up teenager.

"Listen, Josie, I'm not sure this is the right job for you."

Josie leaned forward in her chair and said, "I'm a fast learner."

"I'm sure you are, but I just don't think this is a good match."

"Give me one day to prove myself," she said with surprising vehemence.

Sputnik placed his snout on my thigh. I reached down and petted the little mutt. Jealous, Bub flew over and took his perch on Sputnik's rump. I scratched his head and he puffed out his chest.

I took a deep breath. "All right, Josie, I'll give you a one-day trial run."

"Thank you."

Goddamn it.

FIVE

THE WEATHER WAS STILL crummy the next day—a high gray sky, limp drizzle—but I still got a charge driving over the Kingston-Rhinecliff Bridge and looking down at the Hudson, so wide and slow that it looked more like a lake, the hills on either side dotted with big houses and small towns, cement plants and power lines. I'd discovered the area during my sixteenth summer, when I'd fallen madly in love with a songwriter/poet/lunatic twice my age whom I'd met in Washington Square Park, and was convinced was an undiscovered genius. Jeremy rented a shack in Athens, a tiny riverbank hamlet, and I spent that steamy summer screwing on a futon, listening to Jeremy compose songs I slowly came to realize were trite and grating, making him Bustelo coffee using a paper towel for a filter, rolling him Bugler cigarettes, and generally being a slave to a schmuck.

Ah, youth.

Not that my judgment got much better with age—witness the Asshole.

But in spite of Jeremy, the valley had gotten to me—the quirky towns, the history, the stone houses, the river, the lighthouses, swimming in cool Catskills creeks. I was raised—if you want to call it that—on the streets of the East Village. It's ironic how provincial a city kid can be, the valley that summer was a wonderland, a visual orgasm, a new world. I felt like I could breathe up here, but it wasn't all pristine and prissy and countrified—you know, women in straw hats buying twelve-dollar jars of jam—there were all kinds of people, it was funky and real.

I reached the east side of the river, turned up River Road, and suddenly I was in one of those Jane Austen movies—old stone walls, sweeping fields, fat cows on fancy farms, gingerbread gothic cottages, gatehouses of the old estates.

I came to a stone wall that looked a little *shabucka*—stones had tumbled loose, lay mossy and forlorn. The field beyond was a choppy sea of high grass and saplings. The wall ended at a drive flanked by two nicked-up brick pillars; only one of them still had its stone urn on top. There was a worn bronze sign on one of the columns: Westward Farm.

I turned down the drive, which snaked spookily between tall trees, with gnarly, overgrown fields on either side—through the dank drizzle I saw an abandoned tractor, a crumbling kennel, creepy little copses of trees that looked like sinister men huddling to hatch evil plots. The only thing missing was Julie Andrews bursting forth, arms spread, singing her joyful British brains out.

The drive went on for about a half mile, took a little turn and— *whoa, mama*—there sat a house that seemed to stretch for a couple of city blocks. Set on the crest of a lawn that rolled down to the river, it was grand and stately as all get-out—until you noticed the peeling paint, missing shutters, and cracked windows. There was a circular parking court in front, with a defunct fountain in the middle of it, and an assortment of old cars spread around, including Daphne's Mercedes.

I parked my Camry and got out.

SIX

THE MANSION'S FRONT DOOR was framed by a columned portico. Too bad it was inaccessible, covered with crumbling terra cotta pots, rusted urns, chipped statuary, and other detritus of a good garden gone bad. Remembering what Daphne had told me, I looked to the left—there was a row of tall windows, one of which had been turned into a makeshift door by the crew from *This Old Trailer*. I walked over—it was ajar and I stepped inside.

I was in a huge high-ceilinged parlor filled with the furniture, art, and rugs that Daphne had showed me. Everything was covered in a thick layer of dust, highlighted with bird droppings, empty wine bottles, overflowing ashtrays, yellowing newspapers. The walls and ceiling were water-stained and sported spots of bubbling, crumbling plaster.

Daphne had said she'd probably be upstairs in her bedroom, so I walked through an archway on the right that led into the main hall. The two-story room was split in half by unfinished drywall. The wall began in the dead middle of the front door and continued right up the *Gone With the Wind*-y staircase. From the other side of the wall I could hear faint echoes of Indian music—sitars and cymbals and chanting.

I started up Daphne's side of the stairway, which curved around and led to an open landing, also cut off from the other side of the house by the drywall.

"Daphne?" I called.

No answer. I set out in search of Daphne's bedroom. The rooms I passed were filled with massive pieces of furniture covered with white sheets that lay on them like exhausted ghosts. Everything was dirty and disheveled, there was so much dust in the air I could taste it, I heard critters scurrying around inside the walls. This was what made my work so cool—peeking into other people's lives. I'd seen some pretty bizarre scenes, but Westward Farm was number one with a bullet.

"Daphne?"

No answer. I came to the end of the corridor and there was her bedroom. It was an enormous corner room with windows facing the river and a carved sleigh bed. I poked my head in.

"Daphne, are you here? It's Janet, Janet Petrocelli."

Nothing. I stepped into the room. Unlike the rest of the house, it looked inhabited. There was a tiny makeshift kitchen—hotplate, half fridge, microwave—in one corner, just outside the open bathroom door. Clothes were strewn around, more empty wine bottles everywhere. The bed was unmade, the sheets grimy and gray, and there was an indent on the mattress that told me Daphne spent a good part of her life there. The room had a peculiar smell—musty, overlain with dirty linen, ancient violet sachets, and something earthy and dank, almost like decaying leaves. I moved closer to the bed—the *Times* Sunday magazine was open to the crossword puzzle and there was a tray that held a coffee mug and a small plate with a half-eaten piece of toast. I felt the mug—did it still hold a faint trace of warmth?

I peered into the bathroom: clawfoot tub, octagonal floor tiles, pedestal sink, all gritty and mucky.

But no sign of Daphne.

SEVEN

Back outside, I made a decision: go ask the hated brother if he had seen his hated sister. Maybe they'd made up over a case of wine or two. I walked down to the other end of the house, where another graceful old window had been turned into another sloppy door. I knocked. No answer. Since the house was bigger than a museum, and there was that Indian music playing somewhere in the far reaches, they probably didn't hear me.

I opened the door and stuck my head inside. It was a cavernous room that mirrored the one on Daphne's side, except most of the incredible old furniture was gone, replaced with stuff that looked like Salvation Army rejects. A couple of beat-up plaid couches faced a massive flat-screen television, and a coffee table was strewn with magazines, tortilla chips, soda cans, candy.

"Hello?" I said.

Just then a little girl of around three, wearing a flimsy sundress, rushed into the room in a state of fevered flight. Without noticing me she darted behind a sofa, in hiding.

She was followed, a few beats later, by a woman in her mid-twenties, eating a Ring Ding and smoking a cigarette. She didn't notice me either. "Where's my little Rodent?" she called.

"I didn't see a thing," I said.

The woman turned to me. She was wearing a short shift, would have been pretty with a little more meat on her bones, had long brown hair and enormous blue eyes that looked oddly blank. She sat on the edge of an armchair, crossed her legs, took a puff of her cigarette, and asked, "Who're you?"

"Janet Petrocelli, I have an appointment with Daphne Livingston."

She considered this for a moment, in a vacant sort of way. "Daphne's my aunt," she said, as if reminding herself. She took a bite of her Ring Ding and raised her voice. "Mmmm, this Ring Ding is *soooooo* good!" She cocked an ear. "This is the best damn Ring Ding I have ever eaten."

There was a pause and finally the little girl crawled out from behind the sofa.

"I want Ring Ding, Mommy."

"Not till you eat your Pizza Pocket," Mom said.

The girl grimaced. "Do I *have* to?"

"No … unless you want a Ring Ding."

The girl exhaled in resigned exasperation and stomped off in the direction she had come. Mom said, "That's my Rodent," and followed the child.

My first glimpse of the parenting habits of the old aristocracy. I checked out the magazines on the coffee table—*Yoga Journal* and *National Enquirer*, *Wrestling World* and *Mother Jones*. Someone had a major Dots addiction—there were at least half-a-dozen

Costco-sized boxes of the rubbery candy. There was a standing hookah beside the table.

A woman of around fifty walked into the room. She was naked. She was also pretty broad and fleshy—you might call her layered—and completely nonchalant. Once I got over my shock (if nudity is so natural, why is it always so jarring?), I thought her body looked sort of beautiful, in an I-am-what-I-am kind of way.

"Hi," she said casually. She sat on a couch and fired up the hookah. She took a deep toke and then held out the hose to me. "Hit?" she asked in a squeaky pothead-holding-it-in voice.

I shook my head.

She exhaled.

"You sure? It's primo shit, Humboldt County. Our dealer FedExed it in."

"Maybe later."

She shrugged, picked up the remote, clicked on the television and found a frenetic Spanish-language game show that featured neon costumes, buxom women, lots of music and screeching, and a confetti machine. She howled with laughter, took another toke, grabbed a box of Dots, and then turned to me with a friendly smile.

"I'm Maggie."

"Janet."

"Dot?"

"Nah, I've got bridgework."

"I've never played bridge."

"Me neither."

"I used to read Tarot," she said wistfully. Then she brightened. "You know what, I'm going to read Tarot again … now where did I put my cards?"

She got up and began to root around the room—I was treated, when she leaned over, to several wide-screen views of her bahunkus. After a slow-motion examination of a desk drawer—she seemed to find everything in it mesmerizing, particularly a paperclip—she stood up and said, "I forgot what I'm looking for."

"Tarot cards."

"Ah, fuck it," she said, and sat back down. "What were we talking about?"

"We ranged around."

"I like you," Maggie said, drawing her feet up under her, curling into the sofa. She had a full face, frizzy hair, and small eyes that twinkled. She took another hit from the hookah and then switched the remote to an animal show that featured some weird nocturnal marsupial scurrying around in infrared light. "Wow," she said, "it'd be cute to have one of those."

"It would."

"I bet you could get one on the Internet. I got a seahorse on the Internet, but it arrived dead."

"I'm sorry."

"I froze it, but then it cracked in two when I touched it."

"Listen, I'm looking for Daphne, Daphne Livingston."

"Aunt Daf?"

"Yes."

"Poor Aunt Daf."

"Are you a relative?"

"What is this, twenty questions?" She looked at me for a second with a wary, challenging expression, then popped a Dot in her mouth and switched the remote to a home shopping network where two bizarro-faced women were selling handbags covered with feathers and bangles. Maggie was rapt for a minute, and then switched back to her Spanish-language game show, which cheered her right up. "I'm the housekeeper," she said.

"Oh."

"Yeah, I hold this place together. Without me, it would all go to shit."

No doubt.

"I go way back. My grandfather was the head groundskeeper. So was my Dad. I lived in the old staff house. But then Godfrey burned it down for the insurance money... I mean there was a fire, and I moved in here. Let me give you two cents of advice: don't mention Aunt Daf to anyone on this side of the wall. Godfrey *hates* her—says he'd like to kill her, chop her up, puree her in the blender, drink her, and then shit her out." She leaned in to me and dropped her voice. "See, when Aunt Daf kicks Godfrey gets *everything*. The land, the house, the contents. There's paintings and whatnot over there that would make your head explode. We're talking *mucho dinero*." She leaned back and shook her hair in a proprietary way. "I get a raise when that happens. Course, that wouldn't be hard, since I haven't been paid in three years!" She roared with laughter and her whole body shook, every last layer.

"Where is Godfrey?"

"From the sounds of that music, he's meditating. You might want to wait, he goes postal when people disturb his meditation. Are you a friend of Aunt Daf's?"

I wasn't sure mentioning the nature of my nascent relationship with Daphne would be too smart—I didn't want to end up in that blender myself. "Yes, we're friends."

"Don't tell Godfrey this, but I like Aunt Daf, she's very ... tolerant. Some people get all high and mighty about me being a nudist, the Central Hudson guy had the nerve to lodge a complaint—*asshole*. If I want to sun my koochie, it's *my* business. Aunt Daf is totally cool with it."

"I ... met a little girl, and her mother, just a few minutes ago. Who are they?"

"You're not from DSS, are you?"

"No."

"Cross your heart?"

"Cross my heart."

"That's Becky, Godfrey's daughter. She moved back home about a year ago ... or maybe it was two years ago. Becky's a pretty girl but she's a little *s-l-o-w*, if you get my drift. She ran away to Kansas City. I mean, how lame-ass is that? Anyway, she met a crystal meth dealer in an all-night laundromat and shacked up with him way the hell out in the cornfields and when his meth factory exploded and blew him into a trillion little pieces, she came home. Meth kills brain cells, you know." She took another hit from the hookah. "Sure you don't want a toke?"

"No, thanks. And ... *Rodent* ... is her daughter?"

"Isn't that Rodent the cutest little tidbit?"

"She is pretty cute."

"Can you imagine—a meth dealer's kid living at Westward Farm? Old Lady Livingston would croak. Course she's already dead!" Then she roared again and switched the remote to a rock

33

video and started to dance along from her seat, raising her arms and shaking her upper body in a joyous jiggle-fest. Then she stopped suddenly and looked at me intently. "Who're you again?"

Just as I opened my mouth to refresh the sieve that was her memory, a young woman in her mid-twenties walked in from outside. She looked casual but pulled together in slacks and sweater, carrying a book bag. She and Maggie exchanged a look of mutual antipathy.

"Hello ... Claire Livingston," she said to me, extending her hand.

"Janet Petrocelli."

"She's looking for Aunt Daf," Maggie said.

Claire looked concerned. "Aunt Daphne lives in the south wing."

"I couldn't find her over there, so I thought I'd check here."

"Daphne doesn't come over to the north wing. Can we talk a minute?" Claire asked.

I nodded.

"How about a cup of coffee?"

"Sounds good."

As she led me out of the room, Maggie called out, "I've got some mac 'n' cheese in the oven, give it a check-see, whudya?"

I followed Claire down a long hallway, through a large pantry lined with glass-fronted cabinets, and into a vast kitchen that looked like Katrina's twin sister had just blown through—sinks piled high with dirty dishes, food strewn around, open cabinets, grotty old pots on the stoves, a slightly rancid, moldy smell. One counter was taken up by an armada of bottles, vials, canisters of vitamins, protein powders, herbal boosters. There was a small television blaring, but there was so much snow the picture was barely visible. Claire switched it off.

"First of all, I want to apologize for this household," she said.

"There's no need."

"Yes, there is. Retarded monkeys wouldn't live like this—but Livingstons would. I really should attack it all, but it's just so overwhelming, and besides: a) Dad and Becky and Maggie *like* living this way, and b) if I did clean it up, two days later it would be right back to *this*." She gestured in disgust. "I do, however, keep my corner clean."

There was one spotless countertop with a coffeemaker. Claire got a bag of coffee from a freezer.

"I'm worried about Aunt Daphne," she said as she poured coffee into a brown-paper filter. "She's always been profoundly self-destructive, but things seem to have spun completely out of control. And she seems frightened, somehow."

"Yeah, I sensed that."

"Since I've been back, I've been trying to negotiate a rapprochement between her and dad, but it's hopeless, they just *loathe* each other."

"You don't live here?"

"Oh, good God, no. I've only been back for a couple of months and I'm leaving as soon as I can. I've lived in Seattle for six years and, for obvious reasons, come home as rarely as possible. But I'm teaching a course in American history up at Bard this semester. It's just a one-semester fill-in, but I'm starting my career and Bard is a nice notch in my belt. Another reason I took the job is so that I could check up on my family, or what's left of it. It's been very depressing. Dad still acts like Napoleon on St. Helena, Becky—who is my twin by the way—has clearly inherited the Livingston gene for what I will kindly call eccentricity, and I just learned yesterday that my father wants to *adopt* Maggie, which would make her my sister. The mind boggles. Speaking of minds, if I stay here a day longer than I have to, I'll lose mine." She blew out air, and gave me an abashed smile. "I'm sorry to unload on you."

"Hey, we all need to vent sometimes."

"Thanks. You're the first rational person I've met in this house. I've just had it up to here, and I'm too embarrassed to discuss this with any of my colleagues at Bard. So, how do you know Aunt Daf?"

"I have a small shop, antiques and whatnot, over in Sawyerville. Your aunt came in. She wants me to help her sell some of her things."

Something flashed across Claire's face—surprise, annoyance, rage? But she quickly recovered.

"Well, she certainly has a lot of things *to* sell. My father's Livingston bounty is pretty much long gone," she said with a bitter edge.

There was the sound of footfalls bounding down a back staircase that opened into the kitchen.

"Ah, here comes paterfamilias now," Claire said.

Godfrey blew into the kitchen—tall, lean, bursting with energy. The guy was a pretty amazing specimen—a full head of thick black hair pulled into a ponytail, glowing skin, clear blue eyes, a taut, toned body. He was wearing khaki shorts, a loose oxford shirt, and looked about twenty years younger than the sixty-something he had to be.

"*Goooood* morning!" he said cheerily.

"Hi, Dad," Claire managed. "This is Janet."

He fixed those limpid blue eyes on me. "*God*frey Livingston, what a pleasure," he said, smiling. He was missing a tooth on the upper left.

Then Godfrey beelined over to the health-food counter and started to spoon odd-colored powders and potions into that infamous blender. This was a serious ritual and he went about it with religious concentration.

"Janet is a friend of Aunt Daf's," Claire said.

Godfrey's lithe body tensed momentarily, and then he turned to me and asked, "How's my sister doing?"

"I'm not sure. I can't find her."

"She often goes for long walks, especially in this weather. She's always loved rainy days, since we were children." He sliced a banana into the blender. "I love Daphne. What's happened to her fills me with a sadness that is cosmic, almost too much to bear." He went to the fridge and got out organic eggs and soymilk. He cracked an egg into the blender. "I've tried to reach out to her, to meditate with her, stretch with her, sit with her, *be* with her. But she won't open up to me. She won't let me in."

Claire handed me a mug of coffee—it came with a little roll of her eyes.

"Her rejection has been very painful. She won't acknowledge my essential self. She won't even look at my Map of the Unknown World."

Claire grimaced.

"Your map of what?" I asked.

"The Unknown World."

Godfrey turned on the blender, and as it whirled he did a yoga-pretzel thing—one leg up in back, arm back to grab it, opposite arm out. All he needed was a little salt. He closed his eyes, got all ethereal—probably communicating with the unknown world.

"Dad's been working on his map since I was seven," Claire explained. "He started it, coincidently, the summer my mother left him and moved to the Australian outback."

Godfrey released the pretzel and turned off the blender. "Claire thinks her father is a kook," he said, pouring his greenish concoction into a large glass. "In fact, my Map of the Unknown World is going to make me famous and rich and restore the Livingston name to the glory it once knew. Not that I care about fame or any other material manifestations." He took a big sip and when he put down the glass he was sporting a fat green moustache. Cute look. "Now, I must get to work. When you find my sister, please tell her that my door is always open … my soul is always open."

Godfrey bounded back up from whence he had come.

"I never should have come back here," Claire said, her jaw tense. "My mother knew what she was doing. That man is a narcissistic, deluded, sociopathic asshole. I've been here for a month and he hasn't even asked me what subject I'm teaching."

"Oh damn, the mac 'n' cheese," I remembered.

"*There's no fucking mac 'n' cheese!*" Claire wailed, racing around and violently throwing open the doors of three ovens. Then she plopped into a chair and began to cry.

I'd walked into the middle of something deep and dark, intense and intractable. The worst part was that I found it seductive. If I was still in practice and had a few years to work with Claire, I think we could have come to understand her family and her place in it, could have untangled some of the mess, at least partially freed her. I was sure that she came back to Westward Farm not for her father or her sister, but for herself—like so many children with narcissistic, unavailable parents, she kept going back to the well, unable to accept the fact that it was dry.

Janet, cool it! You came here for antiques! The Claire Livingstons of the world are no longer your responsibility.

But I couldn't stop myself, damn it.

I walked over and put a hand on her shoulder. "Why don't you see if the college has some housing for you. And maybe check Craigslist."

Claire looked up at me and managed a quivery, embarrassed smile. She got up and grabbed a paper towel, blew her nose and gulped some air. "That's a good idea."

"Well, I should be heading out."

"When you do find Aunt Daphne, please give her my love."

EIGHT

IT WAS STILL DRIZZLING, a gentle drizzle, but it felt good to be out in the open air. It always does.

I made a quick recheck of Daphne's digs. No sign of her. Her car was still in the drive; she was probably out for that walk. I headed around the side of the house. The view from the crest of the hill was fantastic—the river, Sawyerville on the far bank, the Catskills rising up in the distance. I realized I was dead opposite the spot where Vince Hammer wanted to build his mini-city. Not only would his plan fuck up Sawyerville, it would screw up a lot of views on this side of the river.

From where I was standing, there was a path that led down to an overgrown formal garden, and beyond that to some kind of folly or summerhouse. Even if I didn't find Daphne, I'd get to walk and clear my head.

The path was flagstone, old and wide, cut into the slope and flanked by mossy stone walls as it descended. The garden itself had once been grand and classical, but was now overgrown, ruined and dreamy, centered around a pocked stone fountain of frolicking nymphs, highlighted by the defiant blooms of rugged old roses. I imagined it in its heyday—manicured, lawn parties, ladies in long dresses, gentlemen in hats, Daphne's childhood in a gilded bubble.

I headed down toward the folly, which sat on a perch above the train tracks and the river. It was rundown too, but pretty cool—octagonal, stone halfway up, then open, finally topped by an onion dome like a Russian church. As I got close, I saw a flash of blue inside. For a moment I thought it was a large bird. I stopped, focused: it was a robe...a quilted blue robe. Hanging from the rafters.

Daphne was in the robe.

I hurried down the path and stepped into the folly. Daphne was hanging from a noose made from the robe's belt, her feet dangling about three feet above the ground, a chair nearby. Her head hung over her collarbone, her mouth was slightly open, her tongue protruding. Her eyes were open too, but her eyeballs were rolled back and all I could see was white. The expression on her face wasn't that final peace we all dream about.

It was terror.

NINE

It was quiet, wet, the world seemed very still—it was just me and Daphne's corpse.

I was with my friend Lena when she died of ovarian cancer, and my friend Manny when he died of AIDS. Fear at the end is common; death is a scary river to cross. But this was different. I barely knew this woman, and it looked like she'd killed herself. Something had happened in the last twenty-four hours that had plunged Daphne into the abyss. And there she was, hanging from a beam.

What to do next?

I had an urge to climb up on the chair and bring her down, move her body into a more dignified position. But it wasn't my place to do that.

I supposed I should go and tell Godfrey—he probably had champagne chilling for just this occasion. But the thought of going back into that swirling vortex of rage, lunacy, and loss filled me with dread. Still, I really didn't have any choice, did I? I needed a few minutes to get my bearings. So I just stood there.

Then I took out my cell phone and called George.

"I'm standing in a crumbling gazebo in front of Daphne Livingston's dead body. She hung herself."

"Holy shit."

"It's spooky."

There was a pause and then George asked, "Are you sure it's suicide?"

"I hadn't considered anything else."

"Hey, remember, that family is looney tunes. And there's a lot at stake."

I looked at Daphne. I guess it was possible that someone had hauled her body up there, but it didn't seem very likely.

"I'm going to call the police," I said.

"Good idea. Are you okay?"

"Yeah."

"All right, keep me posted."

I hung up and dialed 911. I couldn't take my eyes off Daphne, dead, hanging there in that quilted blue robe. For the first time I noticed a small trickle of blood at the corner of her mouth. And she had soiled herself.

"What is the nature of your emergency?" a woman's voice asked.

"I found a dead body."

"Are you sure the individual is dead?"

"Yes."

"Location?"

"Westward Farm, River Road, Rhinebeck."

"We'll send someone out."

She took my name and asked me not to leave the area.

I hung up, took one last look at poor Daphne, and headed for the house.

TEN

I WALKED IN TO find Maggie pretty much as I'd left her—naked with her hookah, her remote, and her Dots. Rodent was on another couch, pulling the stuffing out of a pillow.

"Hi, Maggie, I need to speak to Claire and Godfrey. And Becky, too."

Even from the depths of her stoned zone, Maggie could tell that something was up. She got up, walked into the bisected front hall, cupped her hands to her mouth, and screamed upstairs, "GOD-FREY! GET YOUR SCRAWNY ASS DOWNSTAIRS! YOU TOO, CLAIRE AND BECKY!"

There were footfalls on the front steps and Godfrey appeared, wearing an ink-smeared smock and a do-rag on his head. Claire appeared from the direction of the kitchen.

Claire took one look at me and said, "Is everything all right?"

"I went looking for Daphne. I found her in the gazebo past the garden, she's ... dead."

The three of them looked at each other. Tears began to stream down Maggie's face, Godfrey tilted his head and his eyebrows went up.

"Poor Daphne," Claire muttered. "How did she die?"

"I found her hanging from a beam."

Maggie let loose an incoherent wail and her tears morphed into a blubbery weeping fit.

Becky appeared. "Wassup?"

"Aunt Daphne killed herself in the summerhouse," Claire told her.

"How come?"

"She was having a bad hair day. For Christ's sakes, Becky, why do you *think* she killed herself? She was a terribly unhappy woman. What is *wrong* with this family?" Claire said, her eyes filling with tears.

"Don't get all fucking high and mighty with me," Becky said, going to Rodent and picking her up.

"I could have saved her, but she wouldn't let me," Godfrey said.

"The police are on their way out here," I said.

"You called the police?" Godfrey said.

I nodded.

"You had no right to call the police to Westward Farm. I don't even *know* you. Who *are* you?" he said.

"I discovered a dead body and called the police."

"Well, I want to see my sister," Godfrey said.

He headed for the door, followed by Maggie, who slipped into a pair of flip-flops and a rain slicker,, Claire, and Becky, who scooped up Rodent.

"Do you really think bringing Rodina is a good idea?" Claire asked her sister.

"Why not?" Becky answered.

Claire lowered her voice, "She's three years old, Becky, seeing a dead body hanging from a beam might not be the best thing for her."

"I guess you know all about raising a kid, huh? You know, Claire, I'm sick of you looking down at me, you and your stupid fucking Ph.D."

"It's not my fault you chose to fry your brain cells on crystal meth. Not that you had that many to begin with ... I can't believe I just said that. I'm sorry. Look, Becky, please, leave Rodina here. Just trust me."

Becky made a pouting face and then put Rodina down on the couch. "You stay here, Rodent honey, Mommy will be back in a few minutes."

We all followed Godfrey outside. He strode around the house toward the garden.

"Oh, Godfrey, I'm sorry, I'm *so sorry*," Maggie moaned, rushing to keep up with him.

Claire reached out and took Becky's hand. "You okay, Beckums?"

"I'm scared, Claire-claire."

"It's going to be okay," Claire said.

All four of them were charged with that strange thrill death brings. I'd seen it over and over in my practice—nothing makes people feel more alive than death.

Godfrey rushed down the garden steps, through its wistful decrepitude, and reached the summer house. We followed him in.

"Oh no, poor Daphne!" Maggie keened on seeing the body, "Poor dear Daphne, poor Daphne, *poor Daphne!*"

"Cool it, Maggie!" Godfrey barked.

"Wow," Becky said, looking up at her dead aunt.

Godfrey climbed up on the wobbly chair. "Okay, girls, I'm going to lower her down. Get underneath and grab her."

The three women gathered under the body and Godfrey began to untie the blue quilted belt that wound around the beam and then Daphne's broken neck.

"What do you think you're doing?"

I turned. A cop in his early thirties was standing there.

"I am restoring to my sister a shred of dignity," Godfrey said.

"Until I'm told different this is a crime scene. All of you clear the area."

"Do you know who you're talking to?" Godfrey said.

"Dad ..." Claire pleaded.

"I am Godfrey Livingston and my family has owned this land since 1732."

"That's great," the cop said. "Now clear the area."

An older, portlier policeman arrived. He looked at Daphne and his eyebrows went up. "Damn," he muttered. He blew out air, looked down, scratched his head. "Godfrey, I'm awful sorry."

"I'm very glad to see you, Charlie," Godfrey said. "I would like to lower my sister to the floor. It bothers me to see her like this."

"I don't see what harm that can do."

The younger cop walked over to him. "Isn't this officially a crime scene? It's being compromised."

"These are the Livingstons, Paul."

"Yeah, but ..."

"There is no *but*, Paul. Now, why don't you help bring Daphne down?"

Godfrey stepped off the chair. Paul shrugged, stepped up onto it, and expertly lowered the body into Godfrey's and Claire's arms. They placed her on the floor. Godfrey sat cross-legged beside her and gently pushed the hair out of her face.

"You must be Janet Petrocelli," Charlie said. I nodded. "Let's head back to the house. I'll need to get statements from everyone. Paul, you stay here."

"Charlie, please, before we go," Godfrey said, "I'd like to make a soul circle for my sister." He stood up and held out his hands. Soon we were all holding hands in a circle around Daphne's dead body, even the two reluctant cops.

Godfrey closed his eyes. "Sister Daphne, the Unknown World awaits you, *peace* awaits you—like when it rained and cook made us cinnamon toast before Mother got addicted to pills and Father got addicted to transvestite hookers and everything got twisted and weird. Come home, Daphne, home to the Unknown World."

I snuck a look around—Charlie looked like one of those people in church who work really hard at praying, Paul was scratching his butt crack.

Godfrey turned his head skyward and went into a bellowing chant—"*WHHHHHAAAAAAAAAAAAA!*" Must have freaked out the birds and squirrels.

He ended it abruptly. Then a hand squeeze went around the circle and everyone opened their eyes.

"I have saved my sister," Godfrey said modestly.

I looked down at Daphne—she didn't look too saved to me.

ELEVEN

I GOT A LOUSY night's sleep—I kept running things over in my mind again and again. That whole crazy household, what George had said about it maybe not being a suicide, the sight of Daphne hanging from the rafters in that crumbling summerhouse, the look on her face. In the morning I felt a vague unease—coupled with an intense desire to understand what had happened and to somehow make things right. It was the same feeling I used to get when a particularly touching client got under my skin. I never quite managed that whole "don't take it home with you" thing that was a prerequisite for a sane career in the psychiatric field.

I dragged my ass out of bed and checked myself out in the mirror. Not a pretty picture. I tended to sleep in the same position—curled on my left side—and over the years I'd developed a long morning-wrinkle that ran down my left cheek and was complemented by a section of hair on the back of my head that stuck straight out. When I was in my teens and twenties guys used to tell me I was "cute." Cute doesn't age well, but I guess my face had some character—as in "character actor." Whatever. Aging ain't pretty, but it beats the alternative.

My place was big, sprawling. The building was built in the 1890s as a hardware store and the upstairs was originally used for storage. It had a loft-like, high-ceilinged front room with a row of windows overlooking the street, and a kitchen at the opposite end. There were three bedrooms, a bath, and a porch off the back. It was about ten times the size of my Brooklyn apartment and I felt like I could breath easier, stand taller—and since I was five-foot-four every centimeter mattered. It had the added advantage of serving as a way station for my inventory, and I played a permanent game of musical furniture.

I made a pot of coffee. It was almost ten o'clock. I like to sleep on the late side. When people rave about how beautiful the world looks in the early morning, I tell them it looks just as beautiful in the late morning. George was picking me up for the town meeting at ten-thirty, and that kid Josie was coming in for her trial day. There was no chance she would work out, but at least my conscience wouldn't bug me.

I gulped two cups of coffee, wolfed down a banana, fed my menagerie, took a quick shower, threw on some jeans and a shirt, and headed downstairs just as Josie arrived at the shop. She had cleaned herself up, and looked nervous as hell.

"Morning."

"Good morning, Ms. Petrocelli."

"It's Janet. And you look nice. All right, here's the drill. Nothing in this store is what you would call a valuable antique, so if people ask questions just sort of wing it. Say it's a nice piece, great color, cool design, that kind of thing. You can knock ten percent off the price of anything, twenty percent if it's over two hundred bucks. Let Sputnik out back every couple of hours. Help yourself to anything in the fridge or the cupboard. That's it."

I was about to head outside to wait for George when the phone rang.

"Janet's Planet."

"We need to talk." It was a woman's voice—throaty and hip, not young.

"Who is this?"

"Esmerelda Pillow. And we *do* need to talk."

"What about?"

"The tides, longing … Daphne Livingston, the life and death of."

"So talk, I have about a minute."

"Tick-tock, tick-tock." She laughed, ironic, knowing—this chick was deep. "No matter how fast we run we all end up in the same place."

"Cute."

"Meet me out at the lighthouse tomorrow morning at dawn."

"Should I bring my *I Ching*?"

That laugh again, with its mocking edge. Then she hung up.

TWELVE

"I'M IN LOVE," WERE George's first words as I climbed into his vintage hearse.

"That was quick. I saw you the day before yesterday."

"That's how true love happens, Janet, you of all people should know that. It's just *POW!* and there you are—two people madly deeply *insanely* in love. Oh God, I'm all tingly."

I'd known George a little under a year and this was the third time he'd fallen madly, deeply, *insanely* in love, so I took it with a grain of salt—one of those fat Kosher grains.

"Who is he?"

"His name is Dwayne. He's an artist."

"What kind?"

"He works in wood."

"So he's a carpenter?"

"Don't be so prosaic, Janet. But, yes, he came to repair my wobbly step—and the rest is destiny."

"Anything else I should know about him?" I asked. George had a way of leaving out salient details if they smudged his rose-colored glasses.

"No," George said, a little too casually. "Except that's he's quirky, kind, soulful, *hot* ..."

"And ..."

"You know, Janet, you're impossible. You just want to piss on my parade ... So what if he's married, it's just a technicality at this point."

"I doubt his wife feels that way."

"I would hope his wife wants him to become who he is."

"You mean *her* husband?"

"If he was getting what he needed at home, I don't think he would have fallen into my arms."

I reached over and squeezed his thigh. "I can't wait to meet him."

"Oh, Janet, he's *incredible*. I'm making him dinner tonight ... if he can find a babysitter."

I just let that one sit there. I'm not into bubble bursting—they have a way of deflating on their own.

"So have you been putting in any shifts at the ER?" I asked.

"Nah. Benedictine Hospital called me last week and asked me to fill in for a few days, but the timing was wrong."

"You don't miss the excitement?"

"Sometimes I do. But these days three-quarters of ER visits are folks without insurance who show up with the flu or a nasty splinter. Not exactly life and death stuff," George said. "Besides, Dwayne is all the excitement I can handle."

I filled George in on the details of what had happened yesterday.

"What if Daphne *was* murdered, wouldn't that be fabulous?"

"George, murder isn't fabulous."

"Of course it is. It's almost like sex!"

I could always count on George to cut to the id.

THIRTEEN

THE SAWYERVILLE TOWN HALL was one of those new buildings that's supposed both to relate to the past and aspire to the future, and fails at both—it was a mishmash of red brick, flagstone trim, a swooping roof, and way too much glass. There was a rowdy crowd out front, lots of signs opposed to River Landing, George waved greetings to his compatriots. He loved all this—the fight, the passion, the camaraderie, and most of all the attention.

A small, hirsute male *creature* suddenly appeared and jumped up onto George, wrapping himself around his torso. With an explosion of matted hair that hadn't been washed in a decade or so, a matching beard, filthy bare feet, and wearing a costume left over from a dinner theater production of *Oliver*, he was a cross between an organ grinder's monkey and a midget hippie with a Messiah complex.

"Janet, this is Mad John," George said, grinning.

"Jaaaaaa-*net!*" Mad John said with a mad smile. Not a lot of tooth action there. He planted a big wet kiss on George's cheek and said, "I love Georgie!"

"Ready to face Vince Hammer?" George asked.

"Don't worry about that mothafucka—he builds that city, I'll just torch it," Mad John said.

"I didn't hear that," George said.

"What are they going to do? Throw me in the loony bin?" Mad John roared, rocking back and forth, rocking George right along with him. Then he leapt down and starting jumping up and down like an ecstatic Ritalin-addled three-year-old, singing, "*Don't worry, be crazy.*"

You hadda love him.

Suddenly there was a commotion: Vince Hammer was making his arrival, climbing out of a fat silver SUV. He was tall, handsome, mid-thirties, over-groomed with shiny black hair and glowing skin, surrounded by aides and attorneys. Most of the crowd were adversaries, but Hammer's M.O. was to kill them with charisma—he beamed, exchanged mock-folksy greetings. The guy was like margarine. I wondered why anybody ever bought this kind of bullshit—and then he caught my eye and smiled at me. Think Bill Clinton meets George Clooney.

The city council chamber was jammed, so we stood in the back. The crowd was a Hudson Valley mix of country folk, townies, suburbanites, artsy-crafties, old hippies, bright young things, and a couple of loose screws who probably thought they were there to watch a movie. Mad John crawled down the aisle and sat cross-legged on the floor up front. The five town supervisors sat at a raised table.

"Janet, this is Helen Bearse," George said, introducing the woman standing next to us. "She's a realtor in town."

Helen looked to be in her mid-fifties, small, thin, toned, wearing a stylish beige dress and a fair amount of country-chic jewelry—large stones in geometric silver settings.

"This is going to be a tough one," Helen said. "Vince Hammer has *a lot* of dough, and he's very smooth." She nodded toward the supervisors. "The two on the left are in Hammer's pocket, the two on the right are on our side, the one in the middle—Beth Rogers—is going to swing this thing one way or the other."

Beth Rogers was bespectacled, middle-aged, with shortish gray hair, an erect posture, wearing a blouse and cardigan. She was making notes on a legal pad, looking every inch a librarian—except for that racy vermilion lipstick. Hmmm.

One of the supervisors opened the meeting, explained that there was going to be a presentation by Mr. Hammer, testimony from experts, and then an open mike. He introduced Hammer, who loped to the front of the room and gave us an aw-shucks smile, his eyes twinkling with warmth and sincerity. He waited for the room to settle before be began.

"It's a sacred responsibility, isn't it? To protect this glorious valley that we all love," he began in a honeyed baritone. "A responsibility to our children, and their children. I fulfill that trust by providing harmonious, organic environments for people to live in, work in, play in, *grow* in."

"*Waah-naa!*" Mad John let loose a loud weird high-pitched sound that was part laugh, part snort, part honk—all crazy. Hammer looked down at him, rattled for a moment.

"*Yes!*" George exulted.

"I'd like to show a little movie I made that features an exact rendering of River Landing," Hammer said. "I call it *Through the Eyes of an Eagle.*"

The lights dimmed. Two enormous monitors on either side of the room came on, a lush instrumental version of *This Land Is Your Land* swelled, and we were treated to a panoramic, eagle's-eye view of the Hudson Valley. As the sun rose in the east over the Taconics, the valley was bathed in radiant light and the bird flew over small towns and large estates, lighthouses and bridges, before swooping down to Sawyerville, so close that you could see every building and landmark—and there, on the banks of the river, was a harmonious, organic, digitally created, amazingly lifelike rendering of River Landing. The eagle flew over walkways that wound through a sylvan landscape dotted with ponds, birches, hillocks, and breathtaking river views. Directly across the river sat Westward Farm. The bird flew out over the river in an exhilarating final shot. Fade to black.

The lights came up.

Vince Hammer stood there in righteous silence, biting his lower lip, his eyes filled with reverence. "How blessed are we?" he asked in a beatific whisper.

"*Waah-naa!*"

Vince shot Mad John another rattled glance, but quickly recovered and said, "Did you notice that magnificent estate on the east bank? That's Westward Farm, and it's a piece of American history, the seat of the Livingston Family. It's land can never be developed, ensuring River Landing a spectacular view in perpetuity."

Helen leaned into us. "Hammer has had his eyes on Westward Farm for over a decade."

"What do you mean?" I asked.

"He wants to buy it and live there, has made unbelievable offers to the Livingstons, but some of them refuse to sell."

"But if he lived there he'd be looking at his own development," I said.

"He loves that. He wants to be the King of the Hudson, he's planning developments at four other sites up and down the river."

Vince Hammer was just finishing up. "My door is always open, come and talk to me with any of your concerns. Let's work together to protect this hallowed land."

"*Waah-naa!*"

"I have a request," George called out.

"You'll have to wait for the open mike," the presiding supervisor said.

George ignored him and strode down the aisle, all eyes on him. "Vince, being the good neighbor you are, would you please allow me two minutes of your time?"

Anger flashed in Hammer's eyes, but he smiled and said, "Of course."

George reached the front of the room. "Could we rewind the film to the place where the eagle is flying around River Landing?"

The film started up. As the bird swooped across one of the development's ponds, George yelled: "Freeze." He walked over to a monitor and pointed out a barely visible shadow. "Vince, my man, could you tell us what that shadow is?"

"What shadow?"

"The one with my finger on it … *duh*," George said, rolling his eyes and getting a laugh from the crowd.

"I believe that would be the shadow of River Rhapsody," Vince said, trying to sound nonchalant.

"And what is River Rhapsody?"

"It's a housing unit."

"What *kind* of housing unit?"

"Multi-family."

"How multi?"

"I believe River Rhapsody will contain seventy-five units."

"*Waah-naa!*"

"Okay, seventy-five units. Now if I read your prospectus right, it will have three units to a floor, making it twenty-five stories high."

"Imagine the profound connection to the valley those lucky few living in River Rhapsody will feel," Hammer said.

"Yeah, imagine the profound connection to an ugly condo slab everyone else will feel. Forward again, please." The film restarted. "Freeze! ... Now look over to the right." Sure enough, there was another long shadow. "What's *that* shadow, Vince?"

By now Vince had had enough. He did a little swagger-in-place and said with an edge of defiance in his voice, "That's River Rhythm. It will contain the most luxurious apartments north of Manhattan."

"*Waah-naa!*"

"*What is your problem!?*" Vince barked at Mad John.

"Mirror-mirror on the wall, who's the greediest of them all?" Mad John chanted.

The room burst into gales of laughter, and Hammer gave George and Mad John a look that could freeze a lava flow.

From there, things grew increasingly contentious as folks who both supported and opposed River Landing took to the microphone. Vince Hammer was clearly shaken by the ferocity of his foes. Beth Rogers, on the other hand, remained inscrutable, listening with those racy lips slightly pursed, occasionally taking notes.

The board would convene in two weeks to take a final vote.

George was proud as a gay peacock as we walked outside.

"Me and Mad John nailed that creep's ass pretty good, don't you think?" he said.

"Who *is* Mad John?"

"He's a river rat, lives among the reeds."

"You were both great," I said. "Listen, what do you make of Hammer lusting over Westward Farm?"

"He's a pig from hell, of course he lusts over it—it's one of the most amazing properties in the valley."

"But do you think he could possibly be connected to Daphne's death? Helen Bearse said that some of the family were holding out from selling—what if it was Daphne?"

George just looked at me.

FOURTEEN

I WALKED INTO THE store to find Josie vacuuming. I looked around—mirrors sparkled, wood shone, tchotchkes had been dusted.

"This place looks great," I said.

Josie turned off the vacuum and gave me a proud smile. "I sold something."

"No kidding? What was it?"

"A poster, it said Keith Haring on the bottom."

"Did they ask for a discount?"

"Yes, but I told them no, that he was a great artist and it was valuable."

"Good work."

"Who's Keith Haring?"

I gave Josie a quick tutorial on Haring. Then I called Claire Livingston's cell phone.

"Hi, Claire, it's Janet Petrocelli."

"Hi." Her tone wasn't exactly warm.

"How are you?"

"Holding up."

I waited for her to volunteer some more information. Nope. She didn't.

"I was wondering if there was going to be a funeral?"

"No. But some of Aunt Daphne's old friends, from the local families, are having a small memorial. It's at Franny Van Kirk's chapel Friday at ten in the morning."

"Did you make any decisions about looking for another place to live?"

"Listen, I have to run."

What was that about? She was probably embarrassed that she had opened up to me. I'd seen that happen. People would come in for their first session, or just for an interview as a potential client, and they'd pour their hearts out, reveal their deepest secrets and shame. And then I'd never see them again. Of course, Claire's chilly tone could also be something else—like a message to mind my own business.

But who was Franny Van Kirk? And why did she have a chapel? And most important, why was I letting myself get pulled into this mess? I wanted to study Chinese history, learn to kayak, cook Italian, read *Madame Bovary*. Not get sucked into something that had nothing to do with me.

I looked over to where Daphne had sat that morning, remembered her wistful reminiscences, how fragile and frightened she had been. I didn't have the energy to minister to the living anymore, but I could at least try and find justice for the dead.

The phone rang.

"Hey, babe, want to come out for dinner tonight?" Zack asked. "I've got some good stuff in the garden, I'll make pasta primavera and a gorgeous salad."

I was ambivalent about my relationship with Zack, but then again I was ambivalent about *all* relationships. With good reason. Both my parents had been hippies—they met, naked and body-painted, at a Be-In in Tompkins Square Park. My father was a tin-pot genius, a self-proclaimed East Village *artiste* who was too busy drinking, drugging, declaiming, and screwing to ever start—much less finish—that great novel, painting, play. He acted in incomprehensible off-off-Broadway shows and drove a cab three nights a week to pay his share of the rent on whatever tenement he was currently crashing in. He died when I was ten, when he drove his cab into the East River at three a.m.—his blood toxicology report ran to three pages. I didn't find out for a month.

My mom was about as maternal as a pet rock—she took off to India when I was six and as far as I knew was still a nomad—and I spent most of my childhood farmed out to more conventional aunts and uncles on Long Island, who fought, drank, and hauled their tired asses to jobs they hated. It all left me with a pretty warped view of marriage and family. My first husband was nice, safe, sober, reliable, and had his own star on the Boring Humans Walk of Fame. He was a classic over-correction after a chaotic childhood. When that sad union died a slow death, I fell hard for the Asshole. He was charming, smart, sexy, funny, narcissistic, arrogant, intolerant, promiscuous, and basically viewed marriage (and the wife that inconveniently came with it) as one more step on his march to the Holy Grail of "personal fulfillment."

The truth is I suck at relationships, which is not an easy thing for a therapist to admit. Fortunately I was able to see in my clients what I couldn't always see in myself: the difference between a healthy give and take between two compatible people, and a desperate need to assuage loneliness and be validated in the eyes of family and society. With Zack, my expectations were realistic and my boundaries clear. I was getting my bearings in my new upstate life, and my second wind to carry me through middle age. I didn't want a be-all-and-end-all relationship. Zack was a nice, randy guy—and that was enough for now.

"Pasta primavera sounds great."

"We can have each other for dessert."

Just as I hung up a man walked into the store—around forty, strong but going to seed, the florid face of a boozer, a paunch, thinning blondish hair, wearing jeans, work boots, a sweatshirt.

Josie stiffened and shrank.

"Hi, sweetheart," he said to her. Then he turned to me. "Hey there, Phil Nealy, Josie's stepdad." He attempted a smile, but it came out all oily.

I stood up. "Janet Petrocelli."

He nodded toward Josie. "How's she doing?"

"She's doing great, she's smart and hardworking."

"She is, huh?"

"And attractive."

"If you like gimps."

"Can I help you with something?"

"Nah, I'm not interested in junk."

"Well, feel free to leave then," I said, coming around the desk and approaching him.

"I just came in to see where Josie was working."

"Well, now you've seen it." I went to the door and opened it.

"Are you kicking me out?"

"Draw your own conclusions."

Just then two women, obviously a couple, walked past me into the store. As they began to look around, Phil Nealy and I exchanged glares. Josie was immobile. I put a hand on Nealy's elbow, applied pressure, and led him out to the sidewalk. Booze wafted off him like vapors.

"Listen, do me a favor—don't come around here anymore," I said.

"It's a free country and I'm her stepfather."

"Your freedom ends at my doorstep."

"Is that so?"

"Yes."

"I don't know who the fuck you think you are, but you're messing with the wrong guy."

"Right back at ya."

I looked him dead in the eye. He glared at me before puffing out his chest, spitting on the sidewalk, and walking away.

I went back inside. The two women seemed seriously interested in a set of Russell Wright china, but there was no sign of Josie.

"I'll be right with you," I said.

I went into the back. Josie was sitting in a straight-back chair, gulping air.

"Hey there," I said, putting a hand on her shoulder.

"I'm sorry that I made you hire me."

"You didn't make me do anything."

"You're a nice person and you felt sorry for me."

"Bullshit. I hired you because I need help around here and you seem like you have a lot of potential."

She looked up at me with flashing eyes, "Oh, go fuck yourself."

I suddenly had a massive déjà vu—on all the deeply wounded people I'd taken on, people who needed their psyches rebuilt from the ground up, who had to somehow make peace with horrific childhoods and circumstances, on all the times I'd sworn to myself that I wouldn't get involved again, that I would protect myself.

I just couldn't handle it anymore.

"I'm sorry, but I don't think this is going to work out," I said.

Josie's body heaved, she opened her mouth and a thin stream of vomit poured out.

"Oh, poor baby," I said, reaching for a stack of paper towels.

Before I had time to wipe her off, she jumped out of the chair and ran out of the store. I took a couple of deep breaths and walked out front. The two women gave me a concerned look, but thankfully minded their own business.

"We'll take the Russell Wright," the taller one said.

"It's cool stuff, isn't it?" I said, grateful to have this simple transaction to ground me.

"It is cool, and the price is fair," she said.

"We just bought a little weekend place up in Palenville," her partner said.

"We just love it up here."

"It's magic."

Yeah—black magic maybe.

FIFTEEN

Zack lived in West Sawyerville, right under the eastern flank of the Catskills, in a little cabin next to a stream on a dead-end road. When I first met him I figured that any guy who would buy the place had to have some soul. I arrived to find him strolling around his vegetable garden shirtless, with a drink in his hand, picking the lettuce for dinner.

"Hey, little darlin'," he called. Zack was from Levittown and like a lot of guys who grew up in cities and suburbs but settled in the country, he loved to use twangy slangy language.

He handed me his drink. I took a sip. It was one of his Zack-wackers—basically whatever fresh fruit he had laying around, blendered-up with enough tequila to grow hair on a billiard ball. It was Zack's drink of choice after "a hard day in the fields" (a.k.a. watering rich second-homers' perennial beds), especially during "the high summer months" (which started in the middle of March). For years Zack had worked for a large landscape company, planting trees and building stone walls. Then two years ago he'd decided it was time to "be my own man, be *Zack*." He'd taken a six-week course in landscape design at Ulster Community College and reinvented himself by printing up business cards reading "Zack Goldman, Earth Art." Well, it worked. He had more clients than he could handle, usually eco-earnest types from the city who bought second homes and dreamed of ponds, sweeps of grasses, masses of rare flowers—but who, after hearing the price tag, invariably settled for a couple of perennial beds and a dwarf evergreen or two, all of it tarted up come spring with impatiens, petunias, and geraniums.

The drink went down easy—I needed it. "That's potent stuff."

"I'm a man with potent appetites. And you're one hell of a woman." He leaned over and kissed me. Zack was pretty adorable when he was on his first drink—it was the second and third that were the problems, as he went from endearing to annoying to incoherent to comatose. At least he never got mean.

"How was your day?" I asked, sitting on a stone bench. His property was small, but it was ringed with stone walls and filled with benches, paths, and nooks that Zack had built.

"Darlin', my day was … spectacular. The earth and I worked together to create beauty. It was hard work, earth work, muscles and sweat." He looked up at the mountain, his eyes filled with tenderness and tequila. "It was spiritual work, a work of wonder." I guess he caught my eye-roll because he said, "Janet, sometimes I think you don't take me seriously."

"You don't make it easy."

Zack was a hunk, no doubt—almost six feet of solid beefy muscle, thinning reddish hair, an open face covered with freckles, green eyes nestled in crow's-feet. The package was a big part of the attraction for me. That and the fact that the Asshole had been a self-important, condescending pseudo-intellectual who turned every discussion into a game of one-upmanship. So much of what we do in life is a reaction to our previous mistakes—but Zack didn't feel like an overcorrection. At least not yet.

"My day was good. How was your day?"

I told him about the town meeting, and my suspicion that maybe Vince Hammer was somehow connected to Daphne's death.

"My old company takes care of Hammer's place. It's outside Woodstock, up on Ohayo Mountain. Amazing place, views almost all the way down to the city, they say he spent like ten million building it."

Suddenly a battered red pickup plastered with bumper sticks—"Pray for Whirled Peas," "Honk if You Love Silence," "I'd Rather be Fartin'"—came to a roaring stop in Zack's drive. I steeled myself as the driver's door flew open and a giant burst out.

"The Moooose is looooose!" he bellowed, before galumphing across the lawn and chest-butting with Zack.

"Dude!"

"Fucker!"

"Freak!"

"Loser!"

Male bonding is so erudite.

The giant turned to me. "And there's the Janster! How's it goin', hip sister?"

Moose LaRue was Zack's best friend—a rowdy, six-foot-six fellow landscaper who could "lift a tree ball with a single arm."

"I'm okay, how are you, Moose?"

"The Moose be groovin'! Hey listen—cool news! I bought a boat!"

"No shit," Zack said.

"Yeah, so we can go out drinkin'—I mean fishin'—on the river."

The two of them roared some more.

"Hey listen, Moose, Zack was telling me you take care of Vince Hammer's place," I said.

"Yeah. The man is a solid-gold superfreak."

"You've met him?"

"Hell, yeah. He's one of these rich assholes who has to prove how down-home he is by making nice with his slaves. He's a total dick. Speaking of dick, he can't keep it in his pants. It used to be like the Playboy mansion around there."

"Say more."

"There was a different babe on his arm every time I saw him. Sometimes one on each arm. Cat liked to party. One day I was there doing cleanup and this chick comes out of the house starkers—the bod, Zack man, the bod. She says she wants to take a swim, then she asks me my name. When I tell her, she says 'is it true what they say about moose?' Pretty soon we're in the pool together and she's practicing her underwater humming skills." The boys roared yet again. "Hey, is that a Zackwacker?"

Zack handed him the drink and he downed it in one long swallow.

"But lately there's been just one lady there. Marcella Sedgwick. She is *fierce*. Fuckin' knockout. High-class bitch won't give me the time of day. She's cleaned the place up, a lot less partying. I think they're getting serious. So, amigo, want to go out on the river this weekend?"

"Hell, yes."

"Moose, if River Landing gets built, is your company going to do the landscaping?" I asked.

"We'll do the real work, Hammer hired some fancy-ass Italian company to design the 'scape. He walked my boss and a couple of us grunts around the place, wants it to be a 'work of art'. Give me a fucking break—take away a few bells and whistles and you've got another cheesy townhouse development. I'll tell you another thing—the man is fucking obsessed with that property across the river."

"Westward Farm?"

"Bingo. He kept pointing it out, was practically salivating, called it 'the crown jewel of the Hudson'."

"You want to stay for dinner, Moose?" Zack asked, pulling up a head of red lettuce.

"Not if you're serving rabbit food. Naw, I gotta split. See you Saturday."

He galumphed back to his truck and roared away.

"I hope you're hungry," Zack said as we headed into the cabin.

"Starving."

He slipped in a Phish CD, put a pot of water on the stove, and started to chop vegetables.

"Speaking of obsession," I said, "I'm getting obsessed with Daphne's death."

"Do you really want to get involved?"

"I think I already am."

73

"I thought your big thing up here was keeping out of other people's business."

"I can't just walk away."

Sitting there watching Zack cook, listening to the mellow music on a soft evening in the shadow of the mountain, I should have been relaxed—after all, this was just the kind of life I'd moved upstate for. Instead I felt it rising through my chest, up my spine—that seductive mix of adrenaline, apprehension, anticipation.

"Turn off that water," I said to Zack.

He looked at me, perplexed.

"Just turn it off."

He did. I got up, took his hand, and hauled him to the bedroom.

SIXTEEN

I PULLED INTO THE Sawyerville lighthouse parking lot and Sputnik and I got out. The pre-dawn air was foggy, gray and thick, with a clammy chill—it was going to be a humid day. It was years since I'd been up at this hour and it felt weird, like everything was suspended. We were the only car in the lot. The lighthouse sat at the end of a long, sandy finger of land that jutted out into the river; the Hudson was tidal, even this far up, and at high tide the trail was wet. We set out, Sputnik in high spirits at our adventure, me a little more wary.

This was one of my favorite walks, through woods dripping with vines, along shoreline beaches, over boardwalks, out into the river. In this dim misty light, though, it was creepy—like I was in a horror movie and a mad aunt was going to materialize out of the mist bearing a meat cleaver and a serious grudge. I heard small-animal rustlings in the reeds, the calls of birds waking up, saw a large turtle slip into the water.

We reached the deserted lighthouse, which sat atop a stone base; it was whitewashed brick and except for the light tower looked like a handsome old valley house that had been plunked down in the river. There was a tiny island on the far side; you reached it via a wooden walkway. The island had a large deck and when you were out there, you were really out in the river. The whole place was shrouded in murky fog. Sputnik and I walked around the base of the lighthouse and out to the deck.

"Hello, Janet," that deep, intense voice echoed out of the mist.

"Esmerelda?"

"'Tis I."

As I crossed the deck Esmerelda came into focus, sitting on a bench. She was around sixty and her face was framed with an exploding mass of gray hair that looked like a giant fur ball; she had huge dark eyes lined in kohl and a feathery tattoo that fanned across her forehead. She was smoking a thin brown cigarette, and wearing flip-flops, tight black toreador pants, and a *very* low-cut maroon velvet blouse that revealed the top of the most amazing cleavage I've ever seen. Her toenails and fingernails were fiery red, and she was wearing so much dangly jewelry that she sounded like a demented wind chime. Sexy, weary, deep, dissolute, Esmerelda Pillow was a weird fusion of 1950s beatnik and over-the-hill porn star. Sputnik rushed up to her, she leaned away.

"The dog at dawn, satanic and soul-sucking," she said, narrowing her eyes and appraising him.

"Soul sucking's not his thing, but he'll chew on a greenie if you've got one."

She gave me a feral smile, her teeth were large and whitened. "Comrade," she intoned.

"Do you always get up this early?"

"What makes you think I've been to bed?"

I sat on the other end of the bench. I noticed that her pupils were dilated.

"So, Esmerelda, what's up?"

"Janet, you're still rushing." She ran her fingers lightly over the top of her cleavage—clearly she'd been dining out on that rack for decades. Then she turned and looked out to the shrouded river, taking a deep pull on her cigarette, her eyes filled with mystery, wonder, and emotional histrionics. "Feel the dawn."

"I feel it. It's clammy. Now what did you want to tell me about Daphne?"

She ground out her cigarette on the bench and looked at me. "I saw the best minds of my generation dragging themselves through the negro streets at dawn looking for an angry fix."

"I hope they found it."

"Daphne did."

"Daphne did what?"

"Literal."

"Games give me a headache."

"Let go of your bourgeois affectations."

"I like my bourgeois affectations. I wish I had a few more of them."

"Few of us are what we seem."

Sputnik had disappeared around the side of the lighthouse. I didn't blame him.

"I'm going to go now," I said, getting up.

"Daphne liked to ride the horse."

Suddenly the dilated eyes made sense. I sat back down.

"She had a heroin habit?"

"Pale horse, pale rider. Dark horse, dead rider."

I wished she'd brought along a translator.

"Are you saying that Daphne was killed by bad heroin?"

"Johnny's in the basement mixing up the medicine." Esmerelda reached into her pink leather purse and took out a small round tin. She opened it; it was filled with powdery brown heroin. She dipped the tip of her long right pinky nail into the dope, brought it to her nose and inhaled sharply. Her eyes went to half-lidded and a dreamy little smile curled at the corners of her mouth. She looked at me from far away and drawled, "I'm ready for to fade, into my own parade."

"Now all we need is seventy-six trombones."

Sputnik reappeared, proudly carrying a soggy sneaker in his mouth, which he dropped at my feet.

"An offering," Esmerelda said.

"At least it isn't a formerly living thing. Was it accidental, the bad heroin? Do you know who gave it to her?"

"He lives on love street, lingers long on love street."

"What the hell is that supposed to mean?"

Esmerelda turned away from me, as if she'd lost interest. I guess I didn't rate high enough on her terminally hip-o-meter.

"Listen, Esmerelda, I need a name, an address, *something*."

She lighted another one of her long brown cigarettes and took a deep pull. Then she looked at me with an okay-I'm-going-to-get-real expression. "If you don't pay the piper, the piper won't play ... but the piper will sing."

"Are you the piper?"

"There's an answer in your question."

"There's also an answer *to* my question."

"Pull those little strings and he'll dance for her, he's her puppet."

A fancy cabin cruiser slid silently out of the mist and up to the deck. It was piloted by a middle-aged black man wearing crisp white slacks, a blue oxford shirt, an ascot, and a captain's cap. Dude looked like he should be on Nantucket. "My ride is here," Esmerelda said casually. She got up and nonchalantly stepped onto the boat. "Call me if you want to know more."

"I don't have your number."

"You don't need it."

The boat disappeared into the mist.

SEVENTEEN

Sputnik and I were making our way back to shore when, from a thicket of reeds, I heard: "*Psst! Psst!*" I stopped. "*Psst! Come here!*" As we got closer to the thicket, two hands appeared and parted the reeds—revealing Mad John.

"She's a witch!" he hissed.

"Good morning to you, too."

"She put a curse on me. Then I put one on her."

"Okay."

"Want some coffee?"

"Love some."

He grabbed my arm and pulled me into the middle of the thicket, Sputnik at my heels. The reeds closed behind us and we were chez Mad John. A threadbare oriental rug covered the ground, there was a small camping stove with an old cowboy coffeepot on top, several duffle bags with clothes spilling out of them, and a primitive altar adorned with a Buddha, a Christ, a Frida Kahlo refrigerator magnet, and a half dozen Happy Meals toys.

Mad John sat cross-legged and I joined him. He poured me a cup of coffee in a mug that didn't look too clean. Oh, what the hell—when in the reeds. I took a sip—a little gritty, but the flavor was intense. A box of supermarket donuts stamped Day Old appeared. I took glazed. Went well with the java. Mad John gave Sputnik sprinkles, then picked vanilla frosted for himself.

He took a big bite and said, "She'll be back, tonight, in the dark. He'll let her off the boat, she'll be carrying two suitcases. Then another boat will pick her up." There was a blast of birdsong and Mad John leapt to his feet and answered the bird's cry with a long, melodic whistle. The bird answered, and the two of them carried on an excited conversation before he explained, "That's Fred. He doesn't like dogs. I told him not to worry." Mad John petted Sputnik, who found him very smellworthy.

"What were you saying about Esmerelda?" I asked.

"I know what she has in those suitcases."

"Heroin?"

Mad John tucked his chin and rolled his eyes—I took this to be an affirmative. "She's evil."

"Was she Daphne's dealer?"

"I don't know Daphne," he said quickly, looking away.

"Well, Esmerelda seems to. Do you know where she lives?"

Mad John took my hand—his palm was solid callus—and led me through thick underbrush. We came to a small hidden inlet on the riverbank, muddy and overgrown. A tree grew out over the river and a raft was tied to it. It was constructed of old planks of lumber, straw, reeds, driftwood—and looked about as seaworthy as a pet rock. Mad John grabbed the rope and pulled the raft close to shore. He stepped on board. "Come on."

"I'm not so sure about this."

Sputnik was—he leapt onto the raft, his tail going a mile a minute.

Mad John jumped up and down to show me how sturdy his craft was. What the hell, I knew how to swim. I stepped on board, the raft wobbled but felt pretty solid.

Mad John untied the rope, picked up an oar, and pushed us off. The sun was peeking over the Taconics, giving the dawn mist a pearly glow. When we were about fifteen feet from shore, Mad John steered us south and we headed downriver. This was a whole new perspective on the river, it was like being in a watery green dream or maybe one of those lurid old technicolor movies—the bank a vivid riot of trees, reeds, vines, all of it accompanied by birdsong and enveloped in the iridescent mist.

"We can't stay out long, gotta get back before the sun rises, gotta stay secret," Mad John said. He was a deft raftsman, an athletic little guy, all muscle and sinew. Almost sexy in a weird way—*if* he spent a week in one of those Romanian baths where stout women scrub you so clean your skin bleeds.

We came to a lawn fronting a small 1950s house and he paddled hard to get us across the open space and back into the sheltering gnarl. Sputnik was in dog heaven, racing from one side of the raft to the other, ears cocked, nose twitching, eyes scanning. The sky was growing lighter. We came to a small peninsula. Sitting at the end of it was a ragtag ramshackle house that looked like it took a wrong turn on its way to Appalachia.

The muddy riverbank in front of the house was home to a half-submerged supermarket cart, the lawn littered with car parts and rotting furniture. Mad John grabbed hold of a low-lying branch. "That's where you'll find her," he whispered.

"Esmerelda lives here?"

"Sometimes." He looked over to the east. "We gotta get back."

The current was with us and we made quick time back to Mad John's mooring. He helped me off the raft like a regular little insane gentleman.

As he was tying up the raft he spotted something in the muck. "Aha!" He cupped his palms, reached down, and scooped it up. "Look at this!!"

There was a small green thing squirming around.

"What is it?"

"It's a newt!! The newt we need to stop the mothafucka!"

"Could you back up a bit?"

"This little loverboy is endangered." Mad John leaned down and actually nuzzled the slimy little thing. "Oh, das-a-baby, das-a-baby."

"Shouldn't you leave it where it is then?"

"No! Come on." I followed him back to his crib. He pointed to an empty jelly jar. "Can you open that?"

I did and Mad John slipped the mucky newt in. It immediately tried to climb the sides.

"Look how beautiful!" Mad John said, holding the jar up to my face. The newt was a shimmery green with red and yellow spots.

"Very pretty. But how is he going to stop the motherfucker, and who is the motherfucker?"

"It's verbotenski to mess with this little guy's habitat—and the mothafucka is Vince Hammer."

"Wait … so you're going to release the newt at River Landing?"

"*Hot-cha-cha-cha!*" Mad John said, going into his little jumping up and down routine. "I gotta get a few more first. Then George is going to call the state's herpetologist."

"You guys are brilliant."

"Well, I am."

"I've got to get moving. Thanks for showing me where Esmerelda lives."

As Sputnik and I headed back to the parking lot, he called out to us: "Watch out for her ... watch out for yourself."

And then he and Fred started yakking again.

EIGHTEEN

I WENT HOME, WENT back to bed, woke up at around eleven, ravenous. I headed over to Abba's, where I found George sitting at the counter. Before my butt hit the stool, he said, "Dwayne is *divine*, this is *it*, we're thinking of eloping to Massachusetts."

"Wouldn't that make him a polygamist?

"I'm not going to get hung up on semantics."

"I saw Mad John this morning. He found one of your newts."

"*Shhhh!* That project's top secret. Did he really!?" he whispered.

"Yes," I whispered back.

"That's almost as exciting as Dwayne."

Pearl shambled over.

"Morning, Pearl." Blank stare. "Could I have whatever omelet looks good?"

Pearl pursed her lips and slowly raised her little pad and pencil and wrote... and wrote... and wrote. Then she turned and zombie-walked away.

A couple of minutes later, Abba brought out my omelet.

"You two are not going to believe who called me this morning," she said. "Vince Hammer's office. He wants me to cater a small dinner party next weekend. It's just Vince ... and the Livingston family."

"Boy, he doesn't waste any time," I said.

"The freak wants the farm," George said.

"Badly," Abba added.

"You're going to need some help with that dinner party," I said.

"I am?" Abba said, cocking a skeptical eye.

"You are."

NINETEEN

THE RHINEBECK POLICE STATION was in a small building on the edge of the county fairgrounds. The front room was wood-paneled, had a couple of driving-safety posters on the wall, felt deserted and very 1950s-ish. I stood at the counter. No one appeared. I could see down a hall with a couple of offices opening up off it. I heard a voice I recognized as Charlie Dunn.

"... nah, gimme the suite with all the trimmings. And I want to go out on a fishing charter every single frigging day. Can you folks arrange that for me? ... Good enough. See you next month." Then he whistled happily, farted loudly, sighed in satisfaction.

"Excuse me?" I called.

After some shuffling, Charlie Dunn appeared in the hallway. He saw me and a look of annoyance flashed across his face, followed by a big, friendly smile.

"Hi there, Ms. Petrocelli."

"Hello, Chief."

"What can I do for you today?" he said, reaching the counter.

"I wondered if we could talk about Daphne Livingston's death?"

"Sure," he shrugged.

I waited for him to invite me back to his office. He didn't.

"Can you tell me what your investigation has shown?"

"What investigation?"

"Aren't you going to perform an autopsy to determine the cause of death?"

"You were there, you saw the cause of death. Poor old Daphne hung herself."

"Somebody could have done it for her."

"When was the last time you heard of murder by hanging?"

"So … that's it?"

"That's what?"

"The case is closed?"

"Far as I'm concerned."

"Where's her body?"

"Daphne was cremated. Those were her brother's wishes. I understand he's going to scatter the ashes in the gardens at the farm. It's the end of an era around these parts. We were all so proud of Daphne, before she …"

"Before she what?"

"Listen, I gotta go supervise my officers, we got six escaped ferrets running around downtown."

"Don't you think a possible murder is more important than escaped ferrets?"

There was a long pause.

"This was a suicide, plain and simple," he said, giving me a smug is-there-anything-else-you-want-to-know? look.

"Isn't it possible that someone subdued Daphne, lifted her up to the rafters, tied the belt around her neck, and then let her drop?"

"A lot of things are possible. You know, Ms. Petrocelli, I've known the Livingston family my entire life. They're a distinguished family. This has been hard for them."

"Did you at least write up a report?"

"I did."

"Can I see it?"

"Course. It'll be typed up in a few days. Now is there anything else I can help you with, because I've got to go deal with those ferrets."

"No, I guess not." I looked down at the counter for a moment, drummed my fingers. "Listen, I couldn't help overhearing. Sounds like you're going on a fishing trip."

"Sounds like you're on one right now."

"Touché."

He leaned back on his heels and stuck his thumbs in his belt. "Matter of fact, I am. Florida Keys. Might do a little condo shopping while I'm down there. Pretty word, isn't it: condo. Short for condo-minium. Good thing they don't call them miniums, nowhere near as pretty."

"So you're close to retiring?"

He smirked. "Might be. I'm definitely retiring this little discussion. I got a job to do."

"Go easy on the ferrets," I said.

TWENTY

FRANNY VAN KIRK'S ESTATE was just a few miles south of Westward Farm. There was a caretaker's cottage at the entrance and then the drive wound past a pond, some barns, an orchard—everything was neat, but not manicured. I came to the small stone chapel. There were about a half dozen cars in front—most of them Camrys and Volvos. I parked and got out.

The desultory clutch of mourners mingling on the chapel's front steps were mostly women, mostly ancient, wearing rubber-soled shoes and sans-a-belt slacks—this money was so old it didn't give a shit. Dazed and moving slowly, most of them looked like they were suffering from some combination of early-stage dementia and late-stage alcoholism.

A woman standing on the front steps stuck out her hand as I approached. "Welcome, I'm Franny Van Kirk." She gave me a big smile with a manic edge that screamed *I Love My Paxil*. She had to be in her eighties, with beautifully mottled and deeply lined skin, green eyes, wispy gray hair.

"Hi, I'm Janet Petrocelli."

"A friend of Daphne's?"

I nodded.

"Wait a minute, are you the one who discovered Daphne's body?"

"Yes."

She clutched my hands in hers. "We have to talk. I'm serving tea down in the house after the service. Can you come?"

I nodded.

"Good. Now I better get in."

At the back of the chapel there were two large easels holding boards with photographs and mementos of Daphne's life pinned on them. They told a fascinating story. There she was on the lawns of Westward Farm, a beautiful child living in a lost world. The pictures followed her at birthday parties, on boats, in hotel ballrooms—in all of them she was luminous, enormous eyes, radiant smile. Then she was a teenager and something changed in her face, a tightness around her mouth, a wariness in her eyes—and now she was walking a desegregation picket line, in an avant-garde play, sulking at a family dinner; a yellowed newspaper article announced her arrest for chaining herself to the gates of a nuclear power plant.

Then there was another incarnation—a picture book on the table, *Swinging London*, opened to a picture of Daphne partying with Mick Jagger and Mary Quant. Beside that was a small book of poems, *Movements in the Now and Then* by Daphne Livingston, and a catalogue for a show of her watercolors held in Aix-en-Provence. The other easel held a pulpy movie poster, in Spanish—*Viaje Aspero*, Rough Journey—showing Daphne sitting on an enormous suitcase beside an empty road, looking glamorous, longing, lost. And then the pictures stopped. There was no record of the last twenty-five years of her life, when, according to Abba, she had descended into the netherworld.

I'd had clients like that, people who were fighting hard to tame their demons and stay in the game, but were always being pulled downward by voices buried deep in their psyches—seductive voices urging them to give up, give in, cross over. What made them sympathetic to me was that they did fight, just as Daphne so clearly had.

And then at some point she had surrendered.

"Welcome, everyone, to this remembrance of Daphne's life," Franny Van Kirk said from the altar. I slipped into the last pew. The chapel was chilly and smelled of moist old stone, there were cobwebs in the rafters, and one of the stained glass windows was cracked.

"I'm so sorry that none of the Livingstons are with us this morning," Franny said. The mourners, bunched together in the front pews, exchanged glances. "Those of us who knew Daphne when she was young will never forget her radiance, her passion, her rebellion. When she was growing up, we had an informal reading group, just the two of us. I remember when she discovered Colette. She couldn't have been more than thirteen or fourteen, and she just ignited. One day she said to me, 'Franny, a woman's place is wherever the hell she wants it to be.' After that it was all Paris-Paris-Paris. Well, she got Paris, didn't she?..." Her voice caught and she took a breath. "When she finally came home, back to the valley, I was hoping she had at last found peace ... goodbye, dear girl, goodbye."

Another ancient gal, much less *compos mentis* than Franny, shuffled to the front of the chapel and told vague, rambling stories of long-ago weddings and picnics. Then a bleary priest said the Lord's Prayer and led a desultory little hymn that no one seemed to know the lyrics to—all I could make out were the obligatory "grace" and "glory." That was it. This was a dying tribe that could barely muster the energy to go through the motions.

Everyone filed out of the chapel and began the short walk down the hill to the house. Like Westward Farm, it sat on a rise overlooking the river and was enormous, but less assertive, a warm umber brick with white trim and shutters.

I noticed a showroom-fresh Cadillac parked in the drive, looking out of place. A small old woman was leaning against the car— she had a lumpy, bitter face behind enormous designer sunglasses, framed by a stiff red wig. She was wearing a fancy magenta pantsuit, smoking a cigarette and talking on her cell phone. As she saw us approaching she tossed away the cigarette, got off the phone, and hastened into the far door of the house.

I followed the crowd inside. We moved through a series of stodgy, dated formal rooms—the décor was Early Dust—and ended up in a windowed sunroom that overlooked the lawn, the river, and the distant Catskills.

There was a table set with a coffee urn, a teapot, and plates of Fig Newtons and Lorna Doones. The woman I'd seen out by the Cadillac appeared and took up position behind the table. Close up, she was squat and bowlegged, a little younger than Franny, and had put a frayed floral apron on over her flashy pantsuit. The mourners greeted her with "Hello, Ethel."

Franny appeared and took my arm; the dame had a grip like a pincer. She led me down a hallway, through a pantry and into a huge old kitchen. She opened a standing freezer and took out a bottle of Beefeater's. She poured an inch into a glass and downed it. She looked over her shoulder, lowered her voice, and said, "Daphne *did not* kill herself."

"Okay…"

"She called me the day before she died. It was unusual, she's been very reclusive since she moved back, I rarely heard from her. And she just wanted to chitchat. Daphne Livingston never chitchated in her whole bloody life. She was too busy *living*. Well, we went on about nothing, people we both knew, the old families, and I slowly sensed this desperation from her, a fear. My blood ran cold." She poured herself another shot, went to the fridge and took out a small bottle of capers, shook a half dozen into her gin, and took a sip. "I asked her if everything was all right, and she said 'fine', that she was thinking about doing a little traveling. She was very vague as to where—she mentioned the Yucatan. I was worried and invited her over for dinner the following Saturday. She agreed. But of course by Saturday she was dead." She took another sip of her drink. "I've known Daphne since the day she was born, she was a very talented girl, terrifically alive, but with that cursed Livingston blood. I knew she was in bad shape, but if she was thinking of suicide would she have reached out to me, would she have accepted my dinner invitation?"

"Shouldn't you be telling this to the police?"

"The police are useless. They don't want any trouble, there hasn't been a murder around here in, well, *ever* as far as I know. And I don't trust anyone in her family. That Godfrey is a bad penny. I honestly wouldn't put it past him to murder his sister. Everyone knows he burned down the staff house at Westward Farm so he could collect the insurance. He has a criminal mind, he's half-mad, a degenerate."

"I think Daphne had fallen pretty low herself. I understand she was using heroin."

She took a long swallow of her gin. "Oh, dear. I knew she was in bad shape and I heard all sorts of rumors about her years in Morocco, but *heroin*." She perched on the top rung of a stepladder. "Well, it's not surprising, considering. Her mother was a dear friend of mine. *Vile* woman. She was very jealous of Daphne, wanted to destroy her. Well, she didn't have to. She made sure that Daphne would destroy herself."

Ethel appeared in the kitchen with her antennae twitching. She was so peculiar looking in that fancy magenta pantsuit, just-done matching nails, coiffed wig, and that heavily made-up Mrs. Potato Head face.

"Janet Petrocelli, Ethel Dunn. Janet was the one who discovered Daphne's body."

"I know that," Ethel grunted. "And I say: don't stick your nose where it don't belong."

"That's ridiculous, Ethel, what if Daphne was murdered?" Franny said.

"So what? She's dead, let her lie."

"Lay."

"Yeah-yeah. If you want to stir up a lot of crap, go right ahead. Daphne was a miserable old hag. She probably wants to kiss whoever killed her ... if she *was* killed, that is. I'm not saying she was.

Now I have work to do." She grabbed a fresh bag of Lorna Doones and marched out of the kitchen.

"Pay no attention to Ethel, she's an absurd creature. I only keep her on because she's the only one who knows where the hell anything is in this house."

"Is she by any chance related to the sheriff, Charlie Dunn?"

"Brother and sister."

"She drives a nice car."

"She just bought it. And about a dozen ridiculous outfits. Her brother seems to have suddenly come into some money." She lowered her voice again. "Let's go outside a minute." She led me through a mudroom and out to a fieldstone patio—lawns, the river, the Catskills all spread in front of us.

"What an amazing view," I said.

"I'm sick of it. I wish I could move to Timbuktu. But it's much too late for that." She sat on a stone bench. "It's not that I'm depressed, but I am *bored* ... in spite of volunteering with the League of Women Voters, the Clearwater, the library, and every other goddamn good work within fifty miles." She smiled ruefully. "I wish I could have been more like Daphne. Now she *lived*. In every way. I did what was expected of me. Do you know the only man I ever slept with was my husband? He was a kind man, but he repulsed me. He had this awful pasty little penis, it reminded me of a garden slug." She shuddered and then raised her glass. "Rest in peace, darling." She took a long sip. "Gin is God. But back to Daphne. I want to get to the bottom of what *really* happened to her."

"I feel the same way." We looked at each other, connected. "In fact, I've started nosing around a little."

"Have you really?"

96

I gave her a report on what I'd learned.

"I want to help. Why don't I finance your investigation?"

"I couldn't let you do that."

"I'm rich, Janet."

"But I'd feel beholden."

"Oh, bosh to beholden. If you come up empty, so be it." My finances *were* pretty shaky. "I'll give you a check for five thousand dollars today. Just keep me posted on your progress and let me know if there's anything I can do."

"Are you *sure* you feel comfortable doing this?"

"I'm really *quite* rich."

"You talked me into it."

Franny polished off her gin, stood up, stuck out her hand. We shook.

"I'm doing this for Daphne, of course, but also for me. It makes me feel alive," she said.

"That's a wonderful feeling."

"It's what we all want, isn't it?" She looked out at the landscape. "Suddenly even this tired old view looks fresh. Speaking of fresh …" She raised her glass.

As we headed inside she turned to me. "Do you know the secret of a happy old age?"

"No."

"There isn't one."

TWENTY-ONE

MOOSE'S BOAT WAS JUST a small outboard and felt less seaworthy than Mad John's raft. Especially when it was holding Moose's close-to three hundred pounds, Zack's two hundred pounds, and my ... well, let's not go there.

It was Saturday morning, we had just left the Sawyerville town dock. There was a wind up and the river was choppy, but Moose seemed to know what he was doing.

He cracked open a morning beer, took a slug, and bellowed, "Beer good, good beer."

"Beer real good, real good beer," Zack answered, chugging one of his own.

"Damn, I love being out here!"

"Me too, amigo—land, sky, water, old Mama earth's three essences."

"You left out a slight warming trend," I said.

"Mama earth is pissed at us for fucking her over," Zack said.

"Old Mama earth be ripshit at our fat polluting asses," Moose said. They both roared with laughter.

Hey, in some ways I guess the end of civilization *is* funny.

Maybe.

It took about fifteen minutes to get over to the east bank. It was my first time crossing the river by boat and it was a blast—there were fisherfolk, kayakers, waterskiers. A huge tanker loomed in the distance, the banks rose up on either side, the towns and houses looked like they were in a model railroad set.

Then Westward Farm came into view, sitting atop its sweeping, unkempt lawn with the ruined garden and the romantic folly where Daphne had died.

"Can you bring her in over on the side there?" I asked Moose, pointing to a wooded swath just south of the house. I figured I could get close to the summerhouse under cover of the woods and then duck across the patch of lawn to reach it.

"Sure thing, baby cakes."

Even beered up, Moose was a good skipper and brought the boat to the edge of a nice flat rock. I stepped out.

"Meet me back here in an hour," I said.

"You sure you don't want me to come?" Zack asked.

I hoped my little reconnoiter would be stealthy and silent. "This is a solo gig."

Moose took off as Zack twisted open two fresh bottles of beer.

I crossed the train tracks that ran along the river from Manhattan to Albany and headed into the woods. I've never been rah-rah on woods—nothing to look at but more woods. They were fairly dense but there was an old path.

After a few uphill minutes I was in line with the summerhouse. I figured the odds were pretty slim that any of the mixed nuts up in the house would be looking, but just the same I dashed across the lawn and kept low.

Once inside the summerhouse, I took a good look around. It felt eccentric, Chekhovian, a tattered remnant of a long-ago dream—the perimeter lined with built-in benches, the floor inlaid wood, the domed ceiling crisscrossed by beams, dead wicker furniture. The only sign of recent occupation were two wicker chairs that had a small table set between them. There were birds' nests in the rafters, wine bottles scattered around, the floor was a swirl of bird shit and leaves, everything was covered with a layer of grit. Damn, I should have brought a camera. I was a pretty half-assed private detective.

I climbed up on the wobbly chair that had been underneath Daphne. I guess she could have made it up on her own, thrown her belt around the beam, tied it, and then stepped off. But it no longer seemed very likely.

I began to scour the floor. I found what looked like a fairly recent cigarette butt: Parliament. I carefully wrapped it in tissue and pocketed it.

Time to get back into the house.

TWENTY-TWO

MY HEART WAS THWACKING in my chest as I ducked out of the summerhouse, darted up through the garden, around the house, and through Daphne's makeshift door. The parlor looked the same—none of the paintings or furniture had been moved, nothing had been cleaned up. In the foyer someone had taken a sledgehammer and opened up a hole between Daphne's side and Godfrey's. I crouched down, made my way over to the hole, peeked through. I saw Rodina bouncing on a couch, her lower face covered with chocolate, watching *COPS* on TV—on screen, an ancient gnarled nude guy in a blonde bombshell wig was bouncing up and down on top of a car in a Taco Bell parking lot screaming obscenities and whacking his pud. I love educational television.

I headed upstairs. On the landing, another hole had been smashed in the drywall that separated the two halves of the house. I made my way down the hall. In some of the rooms, the sheets had been taken off the furniture, revealing a Keno twins' wet dream of chairs, tables, and armoires.

As I passed a room, a childish voice called out, "Wanna play Parcheesi?"

I looked in—Becky was sitting splay-legged on the floor with an old Parcheesi board in front of her.

Damn, I'd been busted. But considering Becky's brain cell count, maybe all wasn't lost.

"Not the best time for me," I said, trying to sound nonchalant.

"This was my room," Becky said proudly, sounding like an eight-year-old. Her meth-induced innocence was both touching and terrifying.

"It's a nice room," I said.

"*My room*," she reiterated, slapping the floor possessively.

"Well, now you can have it back."

She lowered her voice and said in an insinuating tone, "I saw you."

"Saw me?" I said, laying on a little innocence myself.

Becky pointed to the window. "Down there. In Aunt Daf's special place."

"Oh. The summerhouse was Aunt Daf's special place?"

Becky nodded.

"What did she do down there?" I asked.

Becky giggled. "Fun things." She giggled again. "Bad things."

I sensed she wanted to say more and so I said nothing. I knew from my days as a therapist that the best way to keep people talking is to shut up.

"She met the scary lady down there."

"The scary lady …?"

Becky raked her fingers through her hair and then fanned it up over her head, opening her eyes wide and demonic.

"The scary lady has wild hair?"

"And big titties," she said, giggling.

"They would meet down there? What would they do?"

Becky gave me a lascivious grin, held out her arm, and mimed shooting up.

"Did you see them?"

Becky nodded. "I went down. I wanted meth. I love meth." She gave me a big smile. "Scary lady wanted to get it for me, but Aunt Daf said no. But now Aunt Daf's dead and we're rich and I get my room back." Then she asked in a hopeful little-girl voice, "Play 'cheesi?"

"No, thanks," I said, "maybe later."

"Eat shit and die."

I continued down the hall and reached Daphne's room. It looked the same as it had the morning of her death. Even the tray with the toast and tea was still sitting on the bed. The toast had sprouted a healthy tuft of greenish mold. Yummy.

Then I saw something I had missed on my first visit: a tote bulging with clothes that looked like they had been hurriedly stuffed into the bag. I rummaged through it and found a small plastic clutch filled with cheap cosmetics, toothbrush, toothpaste, hydrocortisone cream, Preparation H, and prescription bottles for Vicodin, Ambien, Xanax, Oxycontin.

I cased the rest of the room and the bathroom and nothing caught my eye. The whole place made me sad—for Daphne, for all the lost promise in the world. I headed back downstairs. As I tiptoed past Becky's room, I looked in and saw that she had talked a hairless, one-armed doll into playing 'cheesi with her.

TWENTY-THREE

I WAS IN THE parlor when I heard cars pull up outside. Fuck! I ducked under a round table that had a worn old tablecloth draped over it. It was dark under there, it smelled like mold, and there was a small pile of what looked like fossilized cat shit.

"I have to be at Bard in an hour," I heard Claire say as she walked into the room.

"I understand," a woman's voice answered. There was a pause. "Oh my God…"

"What do you think?"

"First of all," the woman said, "you need to have all this inventoried and catalogued. The Livingston provenance will add tremendous value."

"I realize that, but today I'd just like to get your initial impressions. Does anything leap out at you?"

"*Everything* leaps out at me." I could hear the woman's footfalls as she walked around the room, accompanied by quiet gasps and exclamations.

The threadbare fabric covering the table had disintegrated in places, creating small peepholes. I pressed my eye close to one: the woman was in her fifties and looked very *Antiques Roadshow*—coiffed and classy and bright, in an understated way. She was leaning in to examine a small picture. She lifted it off the wall and held it close to her face.

"This watercolor is a Church, it's a study for *Scene on Catskill Creek*."

Claire crossed to her. "Can you give me a rough estimate of its worth?"

The woman held the watercolor back, so that both she and Claire could admire it. "It's so lovely, look at our valley back then, how pastoral it was. Look at the light, just up here—Church was *the* master of capturing our light."

"It's very nice. But can you tell me what it's worth?"

The two women looked at each other.

The appraiser lowered her voice. "My husband and I collect the Hudson Valley school."

"Do you?" Claire said, dropping her own voice.

"We do."

"I see."

"Yes."

"So you buy?"

"We do . . . occasionally. It's difficult, these days . . . the prices."

"It's all the middlemen, isn't it?"

"It is, they drive everything up."

There was a long silence, during which the two women admired the Church some more. When they spoke again, their voices were even more hushed and charged.

"Why don't you take it?" Claire said. "Just as a short-term loan."

"That would give my husband a chance to enjoy it."

"I love the idea of it being appreciated."

"We do have just the place for it. In the library."

"It feels right for a library, doesn't it?"

"It does."

"When it's eventually sold, it would be wonderful if it could stay here in the Hudson Valley," Claire said.

"It belongs here."

"It does."

"All right, if you insist, I will borrow it, just for a month or two." The woman gently slid the picture into her tote. "It will give me a chance to do a little research on Church's latest sales."

"Good. I better get going, I'm teaching today."

The two of them moved toward the door.

"You teach American history, don't you?" the woman asked.

"Yes."

"Such a fascinating history."

"There are really two American histories," Claire said.

"Oh?"

"There's the one we've been taught. And then there's the truth."

TWENTY-FOUR

I waited until I heard the cars drive away before I crawled out from under the table. There was a bright little rectangle on the dingy wall, marking the spot where the Church watercolor had hung. Claire certainly wasn't waiting to cash in on her inheritance. Interesting.

I hurried back through the garden, past the summerhouse, into the woods, and made my way down to the riverbank. Moose and Zack were waiting, sitting in the boat looking snookered.

"Hey, babealicious, how'd it go?" Zack asked.

From their bloodshot eyes and goofdaakus grins, I could tell they'd added reefer to their repertoire.

"Fine," I said, as Moose steered us out into the river. "You guys catch anything?"

They both looked at me with stupid smirks and I could tell their lines hadn't gotten wet. "We had a blast just tooling around," Zack said.

"Boat goooood," Moose said.

"Boat goody-good," Zack answered.

"Boat groovy good."

Zack stood up and bellowed to the heavens, "*Groooooovy boat!*"

They seemed to think this was the funniest line ever uttered—they hooted so hard that we almost capsized. When they finally wound down, they were both winded.

"Fucking fuck-fuck," Moose said in exhaustion.

"Fucking fuck-fuck *fuck*," Zack said, and they exchanged bleary smiles.

We were approaching Sawyerville. I thought of the Parliament butt in my pocket, of the packed tote in Daphne's bedroom, what I'd learned from Becky about Daphne and Esmerelda's rendezvous in the summerhouse, Claire's surreptitious sale. There were a lot of new pieces—now I just had to figure out where they all fit.

"Fuck *for real*, dude," Zack said in a whole new tone of voice, pointing to something in the water ahead of us.

There were two large pale orbs floating side-by-side.

"Looks like a couple of balloons," Moose said.

We got closer.

"Those aren't balloons," I said.

"*Holy shit*," Zack said, his eyes growing wide with shock.

I'd recognize Esmerelda Pillow's boobs anywhere—even with her head missing.

TWENTY-FIVE

BOATERS FIND HEADLESS BODY IN HUDSON

It was late Monday morning and I was sitting at my desk in the shop reading the *Kingston Daily Freeman*. I hated to see my name in the paper, but it was impossible to keep it out—it's not every day a headless torso is found in the Hudson, especially this far north of the Bronx. After spotting Esmerelda's breasts, I'd used Zack's cell to call the police. The Coast Guard appeared about ten minutes later—plenty of time for Moose to toss his stash—and hauled in the body. On shore we were put through perfunctory questioning and sent on our way.

As for Esmerelda's head, it bobbed ashore at Kingston Point beach on Sunday afternoon. Put a damper on more than one family picnic.

I put down the paper, fed Bub a piece of cantaloupe, and considered what my next move might be. Then the bell jangled and a butch black woman in her mid-thirties walked into the shop.

"Janet Petrocelli?"

"That's me."

"Chevrona Williams, New York State Police. I'd like to ask you a few questions."

"You a detective?"

"Yes."

"I'd like to ask you a few questions, too."

She shrugged, took out a small notepad. She moved like a man and was pretty inscrutable.

"Esmerelda Pillow," she said casually, and then she studied my face.

"What about her?"

"You found her body."

"Yup."

"Had you ever met her before that time?"

"I wouldn't call that a meeting. More like a near collision."

"I'd appreciate an answer."

"Don't tell me you think I chopped her head off? By the way, was chopping the head off the cause of death?"

"It's rare to survive decapitation," she said.

I smiled at her but she didn't smile back.

"Once again: had you ever met her before that time?" she asked.

I felt sweat break out under my arms. I fed Bub a piece of a cantaloupe. I petted Sputnik. I wondered if I should lie. I fed Bub another piece of cantaloupe. Then I fed Sputnik one. Lois hated cantaloupe.

"Let me rephrase the question," Detective Williams said. "Your car was seen in the lighthouse parking lot before dawn last Wednesday. Esmerelda Pillow was known to be involved in the heroin trade and to use the lighthouse as a pick-up and drop-off point, often in the pre-dawn hours."

"I'm not involved in the heroin trade. I don't even smoke pot. I like wine, a little tequila now and then. Vodka once in awhile, at parties, that kind of thing. Champagne when I'm not buying. That's it for me."

Chevrona Williams took a step toward me. She was tall and lean and God did she have gorgeous skin and amber-brown eyes. Maybe I should just become a lesbian, a nice neurotic fem. We could vacation in P'town and join a softball league. It would make life so much simpler.

She scrutinized me, narrowing her eyes—I had the feeling she was a Clint Eastwood fan. But it worked.

"Okay, *yes*, I had met Esmerelda Pillow before, once, that morning, at the lighthouse. I was walking Sputnik, this is Sputnik, but you probably figured that out." She just kept giving me that Clint look. "Oh, okay, I went there to meet her."

"Why?"

"*Why?*"

"Why?"

"Um…" I took a deep breath and exhaled. "Because I'm looking into Daphne Livingston's death and Esmerelda called and told me she might have some helpful information."

Williams jotted something in her notebook. "And did she?"

"No. Yes. Yes and no."

"Let's start with the yes."

"She indicated that Daphne was addicted to heroin and that someone may have given her bad heroin."

"And the no?"

"She was so oblique that I couldn't get any hard information out of her. Like the name of who might have done it. Or why."

111

Detective Williams made a few more notes. "So you didn't get any names at all?"

"None."

"And Esmerelda didn't seem frightened?"

"Just the opposite. She was totally cool, in a freaky ancient hipster way."

I saw a slight lessening in the detective's sangfroid. "She was a contemptible woman."

"Oh?"

"She'd hook a newborn if she could. I see junkies in the system every week who we can trace back to Pillow. She once let a shipment of tainted heroin go out on the street. Six people died in Kingston alone."

"So I guess her death is no big loss."

"Off the record I'd call it a gain."

"Did you know she was supplying heroin to Daphne Livingston?" I asked.

"Interesting."

"And did you know that the police chief over in Rhinebeck let the Livingston family cremate Daphne's body before there was an autopsy?"

"I'd heard that, yes."

"What do you make of it?"

"I'd call it shoddy police work, but things work in mysterious ways over there, especially when it comes to the old families."

"You mean they're above the law?"

"It's my understanding that Chief Dunn is going to receive a reprimand. He violated procedure, but he claims that there was no evidence of a crime and he was just following the family's wishes."

"Have you met the Livingston family?"

She shook her head.

"They're a . . . *strange* bunch, and just about every one of them seems happy that Daphne is out of the picture."

"That doesn't make them murderers," she said.

"True. But I don't trust Chief Dunn and, not to cast any aspersions, but you never know who knows who, or who *owes* who, even in law enforcement, if you get my drift."

"You're drifting all over the place."

"It's a tendency of mine."

She leaned in toward me again. "You think it was murder?"

"There are a couple of people with very strong motives."

"Be careful. I've seen people get badly hurt when they start playing detective."

"I found a cigarette butt near Daphne's body." I took the Parliament stub out of my desk drawer and handed it to the detective. She unwrapped the tissue and looked at it.

"I didn't know anybody still smoked these," she said. "We'll have it analyzed. But my words stand: *be careful.* And let me know if you hear anything else." She handed me her card.

"I like your name—Chevrona—it's cool."

She finally smiled. "My mom lived next to a gas station. She wasn't the brightest donut in the dozen. Hey, at least I'm not Exxona."

"You grow up locally?"

"Newburgh."

"There much crime around here?"

"Enough."

TWENTY-SIX

I WAS HEADING OVER to Zack's for dinner—he and Moose had gone out on the boat again and this time they'd actually fished. Zack was going to grill up a striped bass he'd caught. I was wary about eating anything that came out of the Hudson, no matter how safe the state claimed it was. But I was looking forward to dessert—a thick slice of Zack.

It was just dusk and as I drove down a side street I saw Josie Alvarez sitting on a stoop, looking like the loneliest kid in the world. Must be where she lived. I zipped down my window to say hi. Just then her debonair stepfather drove up and got out of his truck, carrying a bag of take-out food. Her shoulders went up, her mouth down.

"There she is—little miss popularity," he sneered at her.

Josie looked at the bag of food.

"I'm so fucking sick of feeding you. Can't you get on welfare?"

Josie said nothing.

"Answer me, you dumb bitch."

Then he slapped her across the face with the back of his hand.

I got out of my car.

"Hey, Phil," I said, walking over.

He turned on me. "What do *you* want?"

I karate kicked him in the stomach. Hard.

His mouth flew open and he collapsed to the ground with a loud, "Uh!" The sack of food went flying.

I knelt beside him. His eyes were rolled up. I gripped his jaw and turned his face toward me.

"You ever lay a finger on Josie again and I'll rip your balls off and shove them so far up your ass you'll think you had them for breakfast. You got that?" When he didn't respond, I gave his Adam's apple a sharp rap. "I said—you got that?"

He moaned and nodded.

I turned to Josie. "Come on." I started back toward my car.

She hesitated.

"*Come on,*" I said.

TWENTY-SEVEN

"All right, there's a bed in here somewhere," I said, gesturing to my spare room, which was an explosion of ... collectibles. Sputnik, with Bub aboard his rump, was following us, both in a state of excitement. Even Lois had come upstairs and hopped up on the dining table, where she was sprawled out pretending not to be interested.

"I won't stay long," Josie said.

"You'll stay as long as it takes for you to find a safe place to live. Now, listen—I'm going out to a friend's for dinner, there's stuff in the kitchen, just help yourself."

"Thank you."

"The best way you could thank me is to get a social worker, find out what kind of assistance there is for you out there, and start to pull your life together. See ya later."

TWENTY-EIGHT

It was Saturday evening and I was in the alley behind Chow, helping Abba load up for Vince Hammer's dinner party. I was semi dressed-up, which for me means a clean blouse and a skirt. Skirts bug me. One reason I got into the junque biz is because it's famous for tolerating slobs and slackers. My great ambition is to be a slacker.

We were loading Abba's station wagon with plastic bins and orange crates filled with food when George appeared, breathless.

"Listen, I just heard some hot skinny on Beth Rogers, the town supervisor with the deciding vote on River Landing. Apparently her husband has a humungozoid gambling problem, practically lives at the Turning Stone Casino up near Syracuse. They say he's got over a hundred thousand dollars in debts."

"So Beth is ripe for a little payoff," Abba said.

"That's the kind of math even I can grasp," I said.

"I think we should pay her a visit," George said. "Just to let her know we're watching her."

"I'll bake her a cake," Abba said.

"Speaking of cooking, I gotta split," George said. "I'm making Dwayne coquilles St. Jacques. You guys have fun tonight."

"I wouldn't call it fun," I said.

"I guess I'm just in Pollyanna mode. Being in love does that."

"When are we going to get to meet this guy?" I asked.

"We're still at that we-don't-need-the-world stage, content just to be together, sit around, watch TV, and, of course, make mad passionate Brangelina love."

Abba and I exchanged a glance.

"I saw that look," George said. "You know, ladies, it's easy to be hard ... wait, let me rephrase that. Cynical—it's easy to be cynical. Some of us still believe in true love. And, for your information, we're all being very adult—I've met his wife."

"That's healthy. And she knows what's going on?" I asked.

"We haven't discussed it yet."

"What did you discuss?"

"Well, we didn't actually *talk*."

"You met, but didn't talk."

"I didn't actually *meet* her. I *saw* her."

"Okay. Where did you see her?"

"Coming out of her house."

"And where were you?"

"Across the street."

"Across the street?"

"I was taking a walk and I happened to find myself across the street from Dwayne's house."

"Did Mrs. Dwayne see *you*?"

"No."

"Why not?"

"I was behind a tree."

"Behind a tree?"

"There happened to be a tree there."

"So you're stalking Dwayne's house."

"Abba, would you please tell Janet that I'm not speaking to her. You can also tell her that if I *was* speaking to her, I would tell her that for a former therapist she's a hard-nosed, insensitive, inconsiderate bitch and I feel deeply sorry for all of her former clients, most of whom have probably committed suicide by now."

He turned on his heels and stormed off.

"I've met Dwayne," Abba said when he was safely out of earshot.

"And?"

"He's one chromosome away from riding the special-ed bus."

"Love is blind."

"In this case it's also dumb."

We drove out through Woodstock—the village green was filled with it usual mix: gray-haired dudes with potbellies and ponytails wearing tie-dyed T-shirts, restless teenagers, rasta drummers of every race, latter-day hippie chicks, and full-blown wackos pacing around having way-deep tête-à-têtes with themselves.

We drove west and then turned up Ohayo Mountain Road. The houses got bigger the higher we went. At the very crest of the mountain we came to an enormous, too-perfect stone wall, bisected by an ornate gate. One of its pillars had a surveillance camera, the other a gold sign reading "Casa Cielo." Abba pulled up to the intercom.

"Yes?" came the disembodied voice.

"Abba Green, here to make dinner."

"Go to the service gate, it's about fifty feet up the road."

Abba let go of the intercom and said, "Well, excuse us."

We drove down to the service entrance, where a less ornate gate rolled open for us. We headed up a long curving drive toward a huge house that sat at the very top of the mountain. The architecture was very Aspen macho, lots of wood and glass, soaring angles and stonework. The grounds were landscaped to within an inch of insane—the place looked like a Four Seasons, with three levels of pools, waterfalls, gardens. But Vince Hammer knew enough to hire the best and it was all pretty stunning, in a strange nobody-really-lives-here way.

My anxiety kicked up a notch. I couldn't believe I was actually going to snoop around this house looking for evidence connecting Vince Hammer to a murder. This guy played in the big leagues, I was just a junque dealer who lived off the grid. My left leg started bouncing, my short hairs prickled, I wished I had a cigarette.

"You okay?" Abba asked.

"Yeah."

"You sure you know what you're doing?"

"No."

We smiled at each other.

"If you need any cover let me know," she said.

"Thanks, amigo."

A majordomo was waiting to greet us in the service driveway. He was wearing a dark suit, young and clean-cut, too clean-cut, almost spooky, the Stepford aide. He had an earpiece in his left ear. Maybe it was just his iPod. Oy.

"Marcus," he said.

"Abba."

"Janet."

"I've got my wait staff arriving in an hour," Abba said.

Marcus nodded. Guy was a regular Chatty Cathy.

He led us into a huge garage carved into the down-slope. There was an elevator at the back and we loaded our stuff in and were whisked up to a cavernous kitchen that could feed the Kazakhstan army with counter space to spare. Then Marcus left us alone—although a mini-Marcus dropped in for a look-see every ten minutes or so. The whole vibe was cold, silent, efficient, and very very luxe.

For the next hour I helped Abba with her prep work. She was serving an all Hudson Valley dinner—cold tomato soup, brook trout pate, free-range chicken breasts sautéed with vegetables and peaches, whipped turnips, salad of every green grown, and apple cobbler with organic ice cream. It all looked delicious but I had zippo appetite—in fact my stomach was clenched like a fist.

The elevator opened and Marcus led off three college-age kids, all wearing black slacks and blue oxford shirts.

"These are my able and adorable waiters—Sam, Siobhan, and Tiff," Abba said, and we all exchanged greetings. "Marcus, the guests will be arriving soon, can you give us a little tour so we know the lay of the land."

Marcus nodded and we followed him down a wide corridor into the dining room. It had a pitched ceiling and a window wall that looked out to the Ashokan Reservoir—glowing cobalt in the early twilight—the valley, the mountains. We seemed to be hovering over it all in a spaceship. The table could seat about forty and looked almost cartoonish set for six.

The dining room bled into a three-story front entry hall that gave way to a vast living room with another towering window wall and fireplace that slept six. The décor was masculine to the point of parody, with leather couches and chairs so huge they almost looked surreal, a balcony above, and a massive bar at one end done up to look like Ye Olde Pub. The whole place had a very Donald Rumsfeld feng shui feeling.

"Bar," Marcus said, pointing. I was starting to admire his economy of speech.

"Sam will be tending bar," Abba said, and he went over to it.

A voice boomed down at us from the balcony: "Greetings to my peeps."

We all looked up and saw Vince Hammer standing there, shirtless. His torso screamed Bowflex, his face screamed bronzer, his hair just screamed—it was meticulously tousled, in one of those just-done-fucking looks favored by pseudo-rebellious young TV actors. The guy was total fromage.

"Here's the drill, kids," he said. "This little dinner is *very* important to me, my guests are people I...*love*. They are *aristocrats*, and aristocrats were the original celebrities. So treat them beautifully. There's a big tip waiting if things go well."

A young woman joined him on the balcony. She was sleek and stunning—long glistening hair, artful make-up—poured into a hot little dress and radiating a fierce predatory intelligence.

"This is Marcella."

Marcella phoned-in a little wave and said, "Hi, gang." She wasn't going to waste any energy on us serfs.

"Get to work, team!" Vince exhorted us, before playfully tweaking his nipples and making a naughty-me face.

When we got back to the kitchen I stood around pretending to help Abba prep and trying to figure how I was going to sneak away and snoop around.

Mini-Marcus appeared. "The guests have just pulled up out front."

"We'll send the hors d'oeuvres out in two minutes," Abba said.

I went out to the dining room and pretended to be checking the place settings. Half hidden behind a candelabra, I could see out to the foyer. Marcus opened the massive double doors for the Livingstons.

"Welcome to Casa Cielo," he said.

Rodent, in a flimsy sundress, immediately ran into the middle of the entry, squatted down, and let loose a stream of steaming piss. No one said anything.

"Who does a girl have to blow to get a drink around here?" Maggie bellowed, marching across the foyer, past the pisser, and into the living room. She had gotten dolled up for the occasion, and was resplendent in an old pink chenille bathrobe polka-dotted with joint burns and accessorized with an exploding-star rhinestone brooch the size of a dinner plate. She was wearing high-heeled cork-soled mules and had pulled her frizzy hair into a band on top of her head—it looked like a mini-geyser was spouting up there.

Godfrey was lugging a huge black tube,."I brought along a tiny section of my Map of the Unknown World, it's only six by forty."

"Wow, cool hotel," Becky said, wandering over to a huge bouquet and asking, "Are these flowers flowers?" There was something touchingly Farrah Fawcettesque about her.

"Claire Livingston, how do you do?" Squeaky clean and wearing a tasteful summer dress, Claire looked like she was on her way to hear Yo-Yo Ma at Tanglewood.

"Vince and Marcella will be down shortly," Marcus said. "Please make yourself at home."

Seeing the Livingston menagerie lessened my anxiety—with that circus in full swing who'd notice that one member of the catering crew was missing for a few minutes?

"Check out this motherfucking view!!" Maggie screamed, and her words ricocheted through the rooms—Casa Cielo had superb acoustics. "I'm tripping out!!" Then she reached into her carpetbag and pulled out a joint the size of my forearm.

Godfrey crouched on the floor and reverentially opened the tube that held his map, Rodina crawled up on a couch and started bouncing up and down, Becky was at the bar ordering a rum-and-diet-coke and flirting with Sam, and Claire was perched on the edge of a chair with a strained smile on her face.

Siobhan and Tiff appeared carrying trays of hors d'oeuvres.

"Wass this?" Maggie asked between tokes.

"Shad roe," Tiff said.

"*Shad*-rack ... Shadrack, Meshack, Abednego," Maggie wailed off-key. Then she stuck the joint between her teeth and started dancing around singing "Shadrack, Meshack, Abednego" and clapping her hands like she was at a gospel revival.

When Tiff approached Godfrey, he wrapped his arms around the tube and barked, "*Get away!* This is *priceless!*" Becky, wearing a loose low-cut shift dress, was leaning over the bar so that her breasts were on full display. and running her fingertips down

Sam's cheek. Claire was munching on a shadrack and pretending she was in a different movie.

Vince appeared, arms outstretched. "It's the Livingstons!"

Nobody paid much attention to him. Except Claire, who stood up and said, "Claire Livingston, how do you do?"

Vince enfolded her in his arms. "You're the only Livingston I haven't met. But I've heard all about you. You're the brilliant one. I'm huge into history. This house was built in 2007. This is Marcella Sedgwick, my lady."

Marcella air kissed Claire. "What a pleasure. I'm so glad we're all able to be together … to get to know one another," Marcella said, oozing fauxcerity, scanning the room and trying to disguise her alarm.

"Are you a Sedgwick Sedgwick?" Claire asked. "Because Clickie Sedgwick was in my class at Brown."

Marcella looked momentarily taken aback, but quickly recovered with, "I *love* Clickie. Distant cousins umptimes removed."

"Well, you certainly have a colorful family," Claire said. "Of course, I'm one to talk." Then she laughed too loudly.

Maggie's corner was starting to fill with smoke and she was still dancing around belting out, "Shadrack, Meshack, Abednego."

Godfrey bellowed, "NOBODY LOOK YET!!!"

"Bartender, champagne," Vince said, nonplussed. This guy was keeping his eye on the prize.

Champagne glasses appeared, corks popped, some sort of hip-hoppy music poured out of hidden speakers. Suddenly the place was party central.

It was time to make my move.

TWENTY-NINE

I SLIPPED INTO THE kitchen, down a short hall, and up a back staircase. Hotel-size hallways led to hotel-looking bedrooms, one after the other. I finally turned a corner and came face-to-face with the master suite. It had double doors, which were open. I walked in. There were so many bells and whistles I wished I'd brought earplugs—wet bar, stone fireplace, hot tub by the window, TV the size of Delaware, mini-gym, mood lighting, mirrors.

There were bathrooms opening off either side of the room. One was all rose marble with gold accents. The other looked like a men's room in a private club, white marble with dark wood accents. I walked in—there was another fireplace, a built-in aquarium, spa tub, steam shower, swinging saloon doors to the toilet, a trompe l'oeil bookcase at the far end filled with leather-bound volumes.

I suddenly felt completely ridiculous—what was I doing in this man's bathroom? I looked at the faux-book titles: *Fanny Hill, Lady Chatterley's Lover, The Story of O*. I was starting to think that Vince doth protest too much. I'd learned in my practice that a guy who claimed to be a super-sexed stud was usually covering up one of the following: erectile dysfunction, bi-curiosity (a.k.a. he's gay), misogyny, premature ejaculation, or a four-inch pecker. I opened the medicine chest—sure enough, there was the Viagra, Cialis, and Yohimbe.

But having a little sex secret was hardly a crime. If it was, the whole planet would be in prison. Maybe it already was.

Cool it, Janet, now is not the time to get all Simone de Beauvoiry!

Then I noticed that the faux bookcase looked a sliver off-kilter. I gave one end a little push and it swung open. A hidden room! I stepped inside and closed the bookcase behind me. My heart, which had been thumping, started pounding.

The room was small and windowless. A safe room. Probably lined with steel. There was a generator, a kitchenette, bottled water, a TV, a safe, a small sofa, and a desk with a computer. The computer screen was black but the computer was on. I clicked on the space bar—a half-played game of solitaire appeared. It took all my willpower not to play it out. (I took solitaire off my own computer because I had a tendency to play, oh, three-to-four hundred games in rapid succession.)

There was a large leather-bound datebook on the desk, inscribed VH. I opened it. The entry for tonight read: "Livingston dinner. Nail it!"

For Monday: "Package to BR." BR could be Beth Rogers, the deciding supervisor in the River Landing permitting. George would be interested in that. I pulled out my cell phone and took a quick picture.

Nothing else looked relevant to Daphne or Esmerelda Pillow. I skimmed through the weeks past—nothing that I could decipher.

Then I reached April 19: EP and DL. Esmerelda Pillow and Daphne Livingston? I took another picture.

I closed the book and tried the desk drawers. All locked. Just for the hell of it, I tried the safe. Locked. There was small gym bag next to it. I looked inside.

Cash.

Lots of cash.

More cash than I'd ever seen in my life.

Enough cash to buy me a small pied in Paris *and* a shack on Maui—no problems, no worries, no people. My breathing grew shallow. I wanted that money. I touched one of the little bundles—oh-so-crispy. I *needed* that money. Vince Hammer didn't. It was probably all earmarked for bribes anyway, dirty money that would be used to grease the slide of the Hudson Valley into Anycondo, USA. More houses, more energy, more of the planet's resources squandered. In fact, this cash would goose global warming and lead directly to the extinction of the human race. Hammer was evil, the devil, he made Hitler look like Mary Poppins with a moustache. I had a *moral responsibility* to take the money. I'd give 10 percent to the Sierra Club. I was Robyn Hood. Besides, he probably wouldn't even miss one or two little stacks.

I sighed and carefully closed the gym bag.

THIRTY

I TIPTOED DOWN THE back stairs and at the bottom I ran right into Marcella, who was carrying a long thin box.

"What were you doing upstairs?" she asked in an ice-cube voice.

"...just gawking."

"See anything interesting?"

"It's all pretty amazing."

She eyeballed me. I tried to look inscrutable.

After a moment, she shook her hair, pouted her lips, and purred. "It *is* pretty amazing, isn't it? *Architecture Digest* is featuring us next month." She held up her right hand and checked out her nails, showing off a *serious* rock. Then she smiled at me. "Kitchen staff isn't allowed upstairs."

Just then Abba appeared, saying, "It's all my fault. I asked Janet to take a peek and give me a report. It's not every day I get inside a house like this one."

Marcella scrutinized us both, then said, "You could have asked for a tour."

"I'm sorry, I should have, but with all the hubbub…" Abba said.

"Never mind." Marcella's face softened. "The dinner is going beautifully. I think it's very healing for the Livingstons. Did you know the family has produced two senators and six cabinet members? But in recent decades, they've been through so much tragedy. I hope that they'll be able to turn a new page now." She handed Abba the box. "These are sparklers. Can you put them into the cobbler when you serve it? The Livingstons have a grand tradition of fireworks. From the 1870s all the way up until the Great Depression, they set them off on their lawn every New Year's Eve. Isn't the aristocracy *fascinating*? With a careful restoration, Westward Farm will rival Monticello." She gave us a bright foxy smile, then turned and walked back toward the dining room.

I exhaled with a sigh. "Thanks."

"How'd it go up there?" Abba asked.

"Mixed bag. How's it going down here?"

She grinned. "Maggie is on her fourths. Potheads are a caterer's best friend."

I helped Abba dress and plate the salad. The waiters took them out and then, anxious to see how the negotiations were proceeding, I skulked down the hallway and hovered just around the corner from the dining room.

"So, my friends, I think we've come to an agreement," I heard Vince say. "I propose a toast to the future of Westward Farm."

"Here-here!" Godfrey said.

"Where-where?" Becky asked.

"What are you each going to do with your money?" Marcella asked in oily excitement.

"I'm going to open a nudist camp for world peace," Maggie said. Then she burst into tears.

"I'm building a museum to house the Map of the Unknown World. Frank Gehry is going to design it."

"Really?" Vince said.

"Yes, Frank and I are in the midst of preliminary telepathic discussions. He's a great guy, very down to earth."

"I'm moving back to Kansas maybe probably. I want to build a shrine where the trailer exploded. It's important for Rodent to know who her father was," Becky said earnestly.

Suddenly Claire got up from the table. "Excuse me." She whipped around the corner and was in my face. "I thought I saw you lurking out here."

"I'm working."

"Working?"

"I'm helping the caterer."

"I thought you were an antiques dealer?"

"Not the world's most successful one."

"You expect me to believe you're here because you need the money?"

"You can believe whatever you want."

"I believe you're snooping around me and my family."

I led her down the hallway, out of earshot. There was a half bath and we went inside, closed the door.

"I think your aunt was murdered," I said.

She flinched. "Really?"

"Yes."

Claire sat down on the toilet and ran her fingers through her hair.

"Who do you think killed her?"

"There are a couple of people floating around who have pretty strong motives."

"Like me?"

I didn't answer.

"You actually think I'm capable of murder?"

"I was a therapist for fifteen years, nothing surprises me."

"If I was going to murder someone it would be my father." She laughed. "Oh, this is sweet. Just when I thought I could see daylight." She tore off a piece of toilet paper and folded it into a tiny napkin on her lap. Then she looked up at me. "You know what? I don't give a shit if Daphne was murdered. I want *out* of this family, and Vince Hammer is my ticket. I'm going to walk away with four million dollars—after taxes."

"You each get four mil?"

"Me and Becky get four, Dad gets six, Maggie gets one. I'll never have to see any of them again."

"I thought you cared about Daphne."

"I care about *me*." She smoothed out the mini-napkin. "Anyway, Aunt Daphne was a degenerate."

"Who's perfect?" I said, giving her what I hoped was a significant look. She picked it up—then dropped it. She stood up, her face suddenly hard and bitter.

"Listen, I'd appreciate it if you'd mind your own business."

"Is that a threat?"

"Why don't we just call it friendly advice."

"It doesn't sound too friendly to me."

"Wow, what a brilliant insight. Move over, Dr. Freud. Let me try and be a little less oblique: If you blow this payout for me, I'll rip your fucking face off. Now if you don't mind, I have to pee."

I headed back to the kitchen. Abba was sticking the sparklers into the cobbler.

"You look a little shook up," she said.

"There's a lot of rage in the world."

The dinner party broke up shortly after dessert, but not before I overheard the three blood Livingstons agreeing to meet Vince at his lawyer's office in Albany on Wednesday afternoon.

THIRTY-ONE

THE POLICE WERE MAKING little headway with Esmerelda Pillow's murder, in spite of questioning people at every marina from Newburgh to Albany. They had determined that she was decapitated by a chainsaw. Not surprisingly, there were marks of a struggle on her body—it was hard to imagine Esmerelda going gently. They hadn't been able to establish where the crime happened—if she had been knocked out on land and then decapitated out on a boat, if the whole thing had happened on a boat, or if she had been decapitated on land and then transported out to the river to be dumped.

I was sitting at my dining table reading all this in the *Daily Freeman*. Josie was over in the kitchen putting away the dishes. The banging and clanging was working on my nerves. Josie had been living with me for over a week now. She was pretty unobtrusive, but I was having a hard time adjusting. After leaving the Asshole I treasured my solitude, my messiness, my non-meals, my odd hours. With Josie around I felt like I had to set an example.

Just like I had to with my clients.

When my marriage was rotting like overripe fruit and every minute spent with the Asshole felt like an assault on my heart and soul, I still had to sit there and listen to my clients complain about their shitty bosses and undermining mothers and offer them my best advice, even though I felt like bursting into tears or screaming at them to shut the fuck up. It was a strain. In my new life there wasn't supposed to be any more of that. Janet was finally let out of her cage, finally free to not be in control all the time, not be so mature and well-adjusted, not to have to set an example. And now here I was, a goddamn surrogate mother.

"Josie, I like to read my morning paper in peace and quiet."

"I'm sorry, Janet."

"And please stop *apologizing* for everything. If I say something like I want to read the morning paper in peace and quiet, just stop what you're doing, or maybe say 'message received' or 'I get ya,' but you have nothing to apologize for. You're trying to be helpful, which I appreciate, but now is not the time."

She looked at me and nodded and went into her room. Sputnik followed. Which annoyed me a lot more than the banging and clanging. Fickle little mutt, he'd have been a dish at a Korean buffet if it wasn't for me.

In case you couldn't tell, I was not having a good morning.

Reading conjecture about Esmerelda's last moments didn't help, although there was a fascination at the gruesome details. There must have been *a lot* of blood. And what did it feel like to saw someone's head off? Did the saw just buzz through, or did it take some effort? And it was definitely overkill. Someone who just wanted her out of the way wouldn't go to all that trouble when a nice clean bullet would do the job. This was a crime of passion. Intense passion.

The phone rang.

"Hello?"

"Janet, it's Franny Van Kirk. Do you think this Esmerelda Pillow business could be connected to Daphne in any way?"

"I think there's a good chance they're connected. According to Becky Livingston, Esmerelda Pillow was Daphne's dealer. She would hand-deliver the heroin to her."

"Rebecca Livingston is not what I would call a reliable source."

"No, but I think she's right on this. I met Pillow. She was upset about Daphne's death for some reason, and I think it was more than just the loss of a good customer. She seemed to take the death personally and to want to avenge it in some way."

"And … ?"

"And that's as far as my thinking has gotten."

"No further progress on Daphne?"

"No, not really. There are quite a few people who are glad she's dead, but that doesn't make them murderers. Do you want your money back?"

"No."

"How's Ethel?"

Franny lowered her voice. "She's on the phone with her brother at all hours, pow-wowing about something, it's very hush-hush. I do my best to eavesdrop, although it's so difficult nowadays with these damn cell phones. I do keep hearing the names Livingston and Hammer."

"Nothing specific?"

"Not that I can gather. But it's awfully suspicious. And Ethel is burning through money, and not wisely. Women who are five-foot-two and weigh 160 pounds should not wear Dolce and Gabbana cocktail dresses."

"I'm surprised it fits."

"What makes you think it does?"

"Well, let me know if you hear anything useful."

"Ditto."

Josie appeared, looking neat and clean.

"I'm taking the bus down to Kingston to meet with my social worker."

"I hope it goes well."

"She's looking for a foster home for me."

"Has she made any progress?"

"I'll find out today. She thinks I should move out of the area. To get away from my stepfather."

"And how do you feel about that?"

An enormous sadness came into her eyes for a moment, and then she willed it down. Brave kid.

"It's okay," she said.

"And what about going back to school?"

"My social worker thinks I should have a place to live first."

"I think she's right."

"She wants me to start learning computer skills. They have special courses."

"That's a terrific idea. It will give you a head start. I have a computer, but I almost never turn it on. You're welcome to use it."

"Thanks."

"Josie, can I ask you something?"

She nodded.

"Your leg. Were you born that way?"

"I broke my leg playing."

"And it didn't heal right?"

She paused. "My mother didn't take me to the hospital for three days. She was very busy, she was working, my father had left her, she was very sad."

"You should talk to the social worker about getting special shoes to even out your legs. It'll lessen your chances of developing arthritis."

She nodded.

Neither one of us said anything. Our relationship felt so tentative. And the truth was I wanted to keep it tentative. I could feel Josie's need pulsing across the room at me.

I kept up my invisible shield.

THIRTY-TWO

I GOT A CALL later that morning from a guy up in Tannersville who said he had some stuff he wanted to sell: he sounded young-ish and hippish, said his stuff was sixties and seventies, so I was interested. My customers didn't want fuddyduddy-frillywilly-cute-sywutsy crap. And I got a lot of calls from people trying to clear out a dead aunt's house, which usually turned out to be a musty mausoleum reeking of mothballs, talc, and ancient body odors, and jammed with Depression glass, freaky little figurines, Victo-rian furniture, and third-rate landscapes. That stuff set my teeth on edge.

But this lead sounded promising, so I got in my car and headed west out of the village—Tannersville was up in the mountains. The day was still and humid, with a low gray cloud cover that was flat as a table. I slipped Charlotte Gainsbourg into my CD player as I drove—her moody monotone went well with the weather. I decided to take one of my favorite roads, the Platte Clove Road, a seasonal track that started in West Sawyerville and snaked up the eastern escarpment of the Catskills. The scenery was spectacular as it wound its way up the Plattekill Gorge, but the road was poorly maintained, with no guardrail and a *loooooong* drop down into the gorge. It was also pretty narrow, so that if a car approached from the other direction, both cars had to slow to a crawl and ease by each other.

I left the village and headed west. It was nice to have something to take my mind off Daphne's murder. After all, buying and selling was what I was supposed to be doing with my life. I was just starting up the mountain road, with rock face on my right and the gorge on my left, when a hulking SUV appeared in my rearview mirror. The windshield was tinted at the top so I had a hard time making out the driver, but he looked big and impatient. Well, if that porker in his pigmobile thought I was going to race up *this* road he had another thing coming.

As I wound up the mountain, he kept getting closer and closer until he was tailgating me. I slowed way down and eased over to let him pass. He stayed right on me.

I was starting to get a bad vibe.

Just then he gave my right-rear fender a *smack!*—pushing me toward the edge.

Holy shit!

Sweat started pouring out of me.

He smacked me again.

I looked down into the gorge—it was *steep* and a long way down, my car would just keep

    plunging

      plunging

      plunging

        until it crumpled into the Plattekill.

I hit the accelerator hard and took off—putting some daylight between me and the motherfucker. Within seconds I was hauling ass around a tight curve, praying that no one was coming from the other side.

The SUV roared up behind me.

He rammed me hard from the left, forcing me into the mountainside. There was a terrible crunch and crush. I spun the wheels out, away from the rock face.

He rammed me again, kept pushing me along the rock, sparks boiling off my front end.

I jammed into reverse—a sickening clang and clunk from the engine.

The SUV pulled back about twenty feet.

Pray he's done with me.

Then it roared forward and nailed me like a bullet—*SMACK!* **M**y head whiplashed, my teeth quaked, my front end crumpled into the rock.

As the sonofabitch peeled past me he tossed out a manila envelope. I got a quick look at him—it was Hammer's henchman Marcus.

I stumbled out of the car, stood there gulping air.

It took me a minute or so, but I realized I was still in one piece.

That's when I started to get pissed.

THIRTY-THREE

Amazingly, my trusty Camry started. I drove it down the mountain to Zack's. He was off creating earth art, but I knew where he kept his spare key. I let myself into the cabin and headed for the television. There was a DVD in that manila envelope and I slipped it into his player.

An empty room, black and white, shot from above. It took me a second to realize that it was Vince Hammer's safe room. Then the hidden door swung open and an ordinary looking woman of around forty ducked in and closed the door behind her. My first thought was that I really had to do something about my posture—I looked like the Hunchback of Notre Dame's long-lost sister. Then again, I was skulking around—who stands up straight when they're skulking? I watched as I looked longingly at the half-played solitaire game. Tragic. More than anything, I looked like one of those sleazy reality-show contestants who are caught by a hidden camera trying to undermine one of their competitors.

There it all was: me photographing the entries in the date book, and salivating over the cash.

I turned off the DVD. And sat there. I really didn't appreciate Vince Hammer's little delivery method. If he'd hoped to scare me off, he'd been wrong. I've got this thing about bullies.

They bug me.

THIRTY-FOUR

I DROVE—GINGERLY—DOWN TO THE dealership in Kingston and within an hour I had a decent used car. Franny Van Kirk's check came in *very* handy.

I drove up Route 28 to Ohayo Mountain Road.

"Yes?" a male voice asked over the intercom at Casa Cielo.

"Janet Petrocelli, I'm here to see Vince."

There was a long pause and then the gate swung open. Hey, this time I was arriving at the front door. I parked in the circular drive and headed up the steps. The door swung open and a dark-suited goon was standing there.

He jerked his head in the direction of the living room. Through the window wall I saw Vince striding around on the huge deck, barking into his cell phone. Nearby, Marcella—in a hot pink leotard—was doing yoga.

I walked out to the deck. Even though it was a cloudy day, Vince was wearing sunglasses so it was a little hard to read his expression, but he didn't seem surprised to see me. Maybe it was just that he was too preoccupied by his phone call, which was clearly pissing him off.

"Tell them we'll counter sue! Tell them I'll hire every lawyer from Albany to Manhattan! And call Speaker Silver's office at the capital. I want to talk to him *today*! That bastard owes me." He slammed the phone shut. "You believe this shit?! They found three fucking endangered *newts* at River Landing and Riverkeeper has filed an emergency suit to stop the whole project. *Newts!* I don't even know what the fuck a newt is! Motherfucking fuck fuck!"

Marcella, who had clearly seen Vince's tantrums before, just kept up her yoga—she was very in touch with her hair and make-up chakras. In spite of her serene expression, I could see her clock my entrance, antennae up. Then I noticed Marcus hanging back, just inside the doors to the deck.

"Is this a bad time?" I asked.

On a dime, Vince collected himself. He sat down and put his feet up on a table. The message: next to the newts, I was a fly.

"What can I do for you?"

"I just thought I'd return this."

I held out the DVD.

"Keep it. In fact, how about taking another copy, there are a lot more where that came from," he said, giving me a loaded look.

"If this one didn't grab me, I don't know why I'd want another."

"Sometimes it takes a couple of viewings for the message to really sink in."

"Oh, I got the message. But don't you think your means of delivery was a little overkill?"

"It wasn't hand-delivered?"

"Yeah right, from a speeding SUV."

"I have no idea what you're talking about," he said in a way that made me believe him.

"Your loquacious friend lurking over there rammed my car into rockface on the Platte Clove Road."

Vince's mouth tightened, Marcella froze in up-dog.

"Marcus, get out here," Vince called. Marcus came out. "Is that true?"

Marcus looked down.

"I hope your dick is bigger than your brain."

Marcella went into down-dog.

"Marcus is still on a learning curve. Get lost." Marcus retreated. "Send me a bill for the car. As for the DVD, maybe we can make a deal."

"I'm listening."

"I'll buy it from you."

"It's yours to begin with, I can't take money just to give it back."

"I like everyone to be happy," he said.

"Even Daphne Livingston and Esmerelda Pillow?"

"For all we know, they could be very happy right now."

A maid came out with a cappuccino on a tray. Vince took a sip and looked out at the view. The deck jutted out over the mountainside, it felt like we were suspended in midair. The reservoir, the valley, the mountains looked muted under that flat gray sky.

"I love this valley," Vince said. "I know you think I'm just some greedbag developer who wants to pave the whole thing over to make a buck."

I was silent.

"And I think you're a nosy two-bit do-gooder who's in way over her head."

"Well then, we understand each other."

"I'm not so sure," he said. "Yeah, I want to make a buck, nothing wrong with that. But I *care* about this place. Did you know I was born down in Poughkeepsie?"

"Interesting town."

"It's a shithole." He took another sip of his cappuccino. "My Mom got multiple sclerosis when I was five. It took her eight fun-filled years to die. You have any concept what it's like to watch your Mom die like that? Losing control of her arms and legs, her speech, her bowels, her breathing. My dad shut down. He delivered heating oil, just went to work, came home, and drank in front of the television set. He was a loser. Mom lived in this crummy room behind the kitchen."

In spite of everything I knew and felt about this guy, I was interested.

"I spent as little time as possible in that house. My bike and my brain were my best friends—I'd ride all day long, up to Hyde Park, even Rhinebeck. I'd look at the fancy houses and think that the people living in them must be so happy. I was a smart kid, I applied for a scholarship to a fancy boarding school outside Boston. I got in. But the rich kids there gave me the cold shoulder. They were all over the minority scholarship kids, but I was white trash. It sucked. I decided to skip college. Well, guess what? I'm richer than any of them. And I'm going to own Westward Farm. And I'm going to give three hundred of the acres to the State of New York with a nice fat endowment and we're going to create the Kathleen Hammer Nature Preserve."

Marcella started *oooommm*-ing.

"Nice way to honor your mom's memory."

"Not really, she hated nature."

"It's also a nice way to earn some good press and a fat tax write-off."

"I'm going to invite my whole fucking class from St. Marks to the dedication."

"Still holding on to that resentment."

"I *love* that resentment—it drives me."

"Maybe too far sometimes."

"Janet, I'm as clean as a whistle in the thistle. Vince Hammer doesn't fuck up. Marcella, will you cool it with the goddamn chanting, you know I have a headache."

Marcella *oooommm*-ed one last time and then stood up. She walked over to us, giving me a lofty little smile.

"Sounds like you two are having a heavy-heavy over here," she said.

"Not really, we're just getting to know each other a little better," Vince said.

"Be careful, Vince has a lot of drive," Marcella said.

"You've got as much drive as I do, baby, you just keep it in a prettier package. This lady is brilliant. She has a B.A. from Yale, an M.A. from Penn, and a Ph.D. in Philosophy from UCLA."

And she was putting all those degrees to good use in that leotard.

"What was your thesis topic?" I asked.

"Ego, Sex, and Money—Kierkegaard versus Voltaire." She gave me a wry smile.

"Weighty, huh?" Vince said. "I love smart women. I think we're a pretty damn good team."

"Rah-rah sis-kum-ba," Marcella drawled. She flipped her hair back. "I think mankind is going through the most profound societal transition since the Industrial Revolution. They've done studies at M.I.T. that prove that the brain synapses of the so-called digital generation fire differently—up to seven times faster—than people over twenty-five. Their eye-brain coordination is unprecedented, as is their ability to absorb and process information and to engage in multiple intellectual activities simultaneously."

"I'm not sure I consider text messaging an intellectual activity," I said.

"We're seeing human evolution accelerating in front of our eyes. What engages and troubles me is the question of where this leaves the developing world. They still haven't mastered the *agrarian* model. Without access to computers, they'll fall further and further behind. We'll see a de facto master race emerge, based not on race or country but on mastery of the language and tools of the digital age. If we don't take action, the consequences for humanity will be catastrophic." She stopped for a quick breath before delivering the topper. "I started my foundation to address these issues."

Vince's eyes were glowing with admiration. "Not only is she brilliant, she *cares*. Get this—Marcella is already on the board at the Bardavon Theater, the Catskill Center for Conservation, and Benedictine Hospital. And she's not just a check writer, she volunteers down at Benedictine. All I can say is: watch out Hillary." He pulled her down onto his lap. "Christ, I love this woman."

Marcella giggled. Very intellectual.

Vince ran his hand down her arm, hip, thigh. She started unbuttoning his shirt. Now they were kissing—like serious Frenching. This was only going in one direction. Whatever happened to manners?

I would have said goodbye, but I was invisible, so why bother?

I started to leave. Marcus was still lurking just inside the doors.

"Janet?" Vince called. I turned. Marcella was licking his neck. "Friends?"

"Yeah, sure, let's do Cancun."

THIRTY-FIVE

"I THINK HE'S GOT the ethics of a gutter rat, but I'm not sure he's capable of murder," I said to Abba as I dug into her chicken potpie. I learned one thing for sure today: getting run off the road gives you a hell of an appetite. And this was a world-class potpie, specked with bits of fresh sage. "His lady friend sure is a piece of work, we're talking fierce."

"From what I've heard, she's really pushing to become a big-time player on the political and social scenes," Abba said. "She has her eyes on Manhattan, and conquering the valley is her stepping-stone."

"Why the hell anyone would want to be a part of those worlds is just beyond me. I'd much rather hang out in jeans and eat chicken potpie."

"Maybe the two murders aren't related," Abba said. "Esmerelda was in a dangerous game. When you run serious drugs you're playing with some vicious characters."

"True."

"And maybe Daphne Livingston killed herself, after all," Abba said. "Heroin addicts tend to be very unhappy people."

"My gut tells me she didn't."

My cell rang.

"This is Janet."

"Franny Van Kirk. Ethel's behavior is growing even more bizarre."

"How?"

"She's taken to chattering like a nattering nabob, I think she's on some sort of happy pills. And she isn't stealing mine, I counted. She's going on about quitting her job, leaving me to fend for myself after thirty-five years. She's putting on airs, and she won't tell me where all this sudden money has come from. She gets very snippy indeed when I bring up Daphne's death."

"You haven't gotten any information out of her?"

"No, but there *is* information to be gotten."

"Any ideas on how?" I asked.

"Liquor tends to loosen her lips."

"What kind?"

"Bourbon is her favorite."

"Why don't I come over tomorrow afternoon and bring you a little present of a very fine bourbon?"

"I like the way you think."

Just as I was getting back to my food, George and Mad John burst into Chow.

"We just got a temporary restraining order on River Landing!" George yelled to the whole place, which erupted in cheers. Mad John started doing his jumping up and down thing. "The judge up in Albany ruled that the project can't proceed until a newt census is completed. It was the newts that did it! And it was Mad John's idea," George said.

Mad John cackled with pride.

"How did you know they were endangered?" I asked him.

"I just knew I didn't see 'em much," he said with a big grin. I was starting to dig his checkerboard teeth.

"This calls for a celebration," Abba said, taking a still-warm blueberry pie off the pass-through shelf. "Free pie on the house. Pearl, get me some vanilla ice cream." Then she turned on the radio to WDST—Bruce Springsteen singing "Born in the USA" came on.

Mad John and George started dancing together in the middle of the restaurant. Penny, a beyond-burned-out old hippy chick who was known for quoting Gurdjieff and giving blow jobs behind the dumpster in the town parking lot, got up and joined them. A cackling, howling ,hooting Mad John grabbed Pearl and pulled her out to the dance floor, where she stood stock still. More dancers joined the bop hop. A couple of bottles of wine appeared.

Just another day at Abba's.

My cell phone rang again. I ducked into the kitchen. "Hello."

"It's Claire Livingston."

"Hi, Claire."

"Can we meet, we need to talk."

"Last time we talked you threatened to rip my face off."

"I want to apologize for that, I was feeling a little emotional. But I need to see you."

"Does it have to do with Daphne's death?"

"Yes. How about at Olana? Day after tomorrow? Mid-afternoon?"

"See you there at three," I said.

I headed back out. Mad John urged me onto the dance floor. I shook my head. I've always been an insecure dancer and my confidence hasn't improved with age. The Asshole said I looked like "a spastic goose" when I danced. Wasn't that sweet of him?

Josie, who I'd left in charge of the store, came into Chow. She had her usual anxious expression, but her eyes lit up for a moment at all the dancing.

"There's a woman in the store came to see you," she said.

"Did she give her name?"

"Detective Williams."

"All right, I'm going to head over."

"Come on, Josie, dance with us," George said.

Josie shrank into herself, tucked her short leg behind her.

As I walked out, I heard George said, "Abba, I think Josie needs a haircut."

"I'll get my scissors."

THIRTY-SIX

Chevrona Williams was standing in the middle of the store holding a couple of files and looking around with mild disinterest—definitely not a junque junkie.

"Hi, there," I said.

She gave me a little smile, showing those nice white teeth, all unforced cool and androgynous elegance.

"How are you, Janet?"

"I've had better days."

I told her what happened up on the mountain.

"Why didn't you report it to the police?"

"I just did."

"This sounds like attempted murder."

"Actually I think it was closer to attempted scare-the-shit-out-of-her."

She smiled again, in that taciturn Clint Eastwood way. God, was she hot. I've never done the lesbo thing, but some women sure do tempt me. I learned as a therapist that human sexuality is a continuum with *every* possible permutation. After listening to people's deepest darkest sex secrets for fifteen years, I'd developed a complex and profound philosophy of human sexuality: *whatever*. As long as it's consensual and there are no kids involved, go for it and leave the guilt at the door. Of course, there are all sorts of emotional and moral nuances when the guy getting gang-banged by a pack of pierced-and-poppered bears happens to have a wife at home who thinks he's at a software conference. But that's a separate kettle from the nookie itself, no?

"Have a seat, can I offer you something to drink? Soda, juice, coffee, tea?" I said, wishing I could have sixty seconds in front of a mirror, just to run a brush through my mop, maybe dab on a little lipstick.

"Coffee sounds great."

Chevrona remained standing as I poured her a cup.

"Please, sit," I said.

"Thanks."

Chick had more class than all the Livingstons combined.

"Did you get the license plate on the car today?" she asked.

"It was one of Vince Hammer's goons. I did something stupid, went nosing around his house and got caught." I handed her the cup of coffee. "I guess I've got a lot to learn."

"That brings me right to: what *have* you learned?"

"Not a lot. Did you have any luck with the Parliament butt?"

"Yes. It has Godfrey Livingston's fingerprints on it."

"Wow."

"I wouldn't get too excited. The butt was found on his property, people still have a right to smoke."

"Yes, but it's a huge property and I found it in the summer-house where Daphne died and it's a fresh butt."

"True, true, and true."

"By the way, why are his fingerprints on file?"

"Godfrey Livingston has a fairly long arrest record."

"For what?"

"Trespassing on government property, disorderly conduct, resisting arrest, that kind of thing. Nothing too serious, he was a political radical back in the 70s. His last arrest was in 1988 for possessing marijuana with intention to sell. Since then he's kept out of trouble."

"Age tends to calm people down," I said.

"I can't wait," Chevrona said, with an ironic undertone that made me think something tough was going on in her life.

"So what's in those files?'

She held up one and said, "Livingston," and then the other, "Pillow."

"How come you have them both?"

"I asked for them. Nobody was doing anything with the Livingston case so it was hard for them to say no. I got exactly the vibe you warned me about—the folks across the river want this disappeared."

"How's the coffee?"

"Fine," she said politely.

"It's out of a can."

"I can believe that."

Starbucks, here I come.

"What are you thinking?" I asked.

"Well, Daphne Livingston died of hanging, Esmerelda Pillow had her head cut off. Two very different means of death, but both are neck-centered."

"So that might indicate a single killer?"

"It's something."

"So you agree Daphne was murdered?"

"I'm leaning in that direction."

"Becky Livingston told me that Esmerelda visited with Daphne pretty regularly. She saw them in the summerhouse together the morning Daphne died."

"Okay, Janet, you have to tell me stuff like this *first*."

"I was about to, then there was the cigarette butt, the coffee, then the files … um, sorry."

"Forgiven."

"It would take someone pretty strong to get her up to the beam. I don't think Esmerelda could have done it."

"It could have been more than one person," Chevrona said, standing up.

"I hadn't even thought of that. Do you think these crimes are going to be solved?"

"They're not going to solve themselves. We know nothing is happening across the river, and there's nobody over here mourning Ms. Pillow. She ran a lot of dope through Kingston. Of course, it's very possible the two crimes are unrelated."

"In spite of the neck connection?"

"Necks are vulnerable places."

I looked at Chevrona's neck. It was long and smooth. I touched my own neck.

"There are a lot of vulnerable places," I said.

Chevrona walked to the door and just as she was about to leave, she turned to me.

"That girl you have working for you?"

"Josie?"

"She's solid."

I nodded.

"What's with her leg? Abuse?"

"Neglect."

"There's a lot of that going around."

THIRTY-SEVEN

I TOOLED DOWN THE drive of Franny's estate with the expensive bottle of bourbon riding shotgun. I just hoped it would work its magic on Ethel. Franny was right, there was information to be had: Ethel had an inside track as to what was happening with local law enforcement, a.k.a. the obstructionists. And the Dunns' newfound wealth hadn't come from a lottery scratch ticket.

Franny came out of the house to greet me. I handed her the bottle and she gave me a conspiratorial look. She led me through the formal rooms to the sunroom, which was filled with books, magazines, and well-used old furniture. It was a warm humid day, the view obscured by a hazy sky, but there was no air conditioning on. Old Yankees love to suffer.

"Ethel, our guest is here," Franny called in the direction of the kitchen.

"Yeah-yeah," Ethel called back.

Franny sat in what was clearly "her" chair, clasped her hands in her lap, and said, "So!" She was quite keyed-up about our little truth-serum scenario.

Ethel appeared carrying a tray that held a teapot with two Lipton tags hanging out and two cups. She looked squat and lumpy in chic black slacks and high heels, a turquoise silk blouse, and a very hip black leather vest. She had on a pouffy red wig, a lot of make-up, and all in all bore an uncanny resemblance to a drag queen impersonating Ethel Merman.

"You remember Janet, Ethel."

Ethel let out a little grunt of greeting.

"Janet buys and sells antiques, I'm thinking of finally parting with a few of the relics out in the barn. But, Ethel, where are the sandwiches I asked for?"

Ethel just gave her a deadpan look—you could practically smell the thirty-five years of passive aggression between these two.

"I asked for cream cheese and olive sandwiches," Franny said.

Ethel mockingly mouthed *I asked for cream-cheese and olive sandwiches.*

"By the way, Ethel," Franny said, "Janet brought me the most marvelous present. It's a new bourbon made right here in the Hudson Valley."

She held up the bottle of Tuthilltown Hudson Baby Bourbon.

Ethel couldn't disguise her interest.

"The guy at the liquor store told me it was the first bourbon ever made in New York State, the distillery is down near New Paltz," I said. "He said that it was 'smooth and dreamy with hints of vanilla and caramel,' and so popular that he can't keep it in stock."

"I think we simply *must* try it," Franny said. "The sun's past the yardarm somewhere in the world."

"Well, if you insist," Ethel said.

"Oh, did you want to join us?" Franny asked.

Ethel gave a disinterested shrug.

"I was looking forward to those sandwiches."

Ethel disappeared and reappeared in record time with a small plate of crustless white-bread sandwiches.

"I'll go get some ice," Franny said, leaping up and heading into the kitchen.

Ethel plopped down on a loveseat.

"Nice outfit," I lied.

Ethel gave her wig a few proud pats and said, "I got it on the Internet."

"I'm not surprised."

"Boy, that one's been a goddamn nuisance lately," she said, nodding toward the kitchen. "Sticking her nose where it don't belong. If she's not careful, someone might bite it right off." She gave a little cackle.

Franny appeared with an ice bucket, which she put on the small corner bar. She put ice into three cocktail glasses, poured in hefty amounts of bourbon, handed the glasses around, lifted hers and toasted, "Chin-chin."

Ethel and Franny both took hearty swallows. I pretended to sip mine—my one experience with bourbon had led to a nightmare two-day hangover. The fumes alone were making me dizzy.

Franny sat back down in her chairl "Well, what does everyone think?"

"Too soon to tell," Ethel said, taking another swallow.

"I think it's outstanding!" Franny said.

The two of them were emptying their glasses at an alarming rate.

"About your antiques," I said.

"Oh, let's not talk business now!" Franny turned to Ethel. "I bet your brother would love this bourbon."

"He might," Ethel said.

"I had a nice chat with him the other day," I said.

"That's not what he called it," she said, polishing off her drink. She held out the glass to Franny and said, "Chop-chop." Then she laughed.

"You see how she talks to me? Like she's the one paying *me* a salary," Franny said. But she got up—a bit unsteadily—and took Ethel's glass and her own over to the bar. As she refilled them, she said, "The tyranny of the serving class is one of humanity's great unwritten stories."

"What are you babbling on about, you old bat?"

Franny handed Ethel back her glass and they both swallowed. "Nothing, just the thousands of times you've robbed me of my dignity over the years."

"You haven't got any goddamn dignity *to* rob."

Franny swayed over to me and hissed, "She lurks around corners, steals the change from the bottom of my purse, and once she fed me dog food!"

"And she ate it!" Ethel cried in triumph, before laughing like a stevedore.

"You're ghastly!!"

Ethel gathered herself, raised her chin, and said matter-of-factly, "Alpo beef chunks in gravy. I told you it was an old family recipe—*and you believed me!*"

It was *Upstairs Downstairs* at *Whatever Happened to Baby Jane*'s house.

Franny turned on me and cried with frustration, "See—she wins, she always wins."

I debated whether to wade into this *folie a deux*—after all, I had done some couples counseling—but decided to try and move things toward the matter at hand.

"Ethel, you and your brother are doing so well these days," I said casually.

"You noticed," she said, before taking a big swig of her drink, smiling at Franny, and going in for the kill. "You're pathetic, and you *smell*. You've smelled for thirty-five years." She turned to me. "She hates to bathe, she only showers once a month. *In the summer*. She *never* washes from October to May."

Franny turned to me and said, a bit sheepishly, "I don't *like* being wet, it gives me the wee-woos."

"But you don't mind stinking like old cheese. Everybody knows you smell. I once asked your husband if he'd seen you and he said, 'No, I haven't smelled her.' Oh we had a good laugh on that one! And she picks her nose when she does her stupid crossword puzzle."

"Oh you-you-*you*-YOU!!!" Franny cried.

"Oh shut up and make yourself useful," Ethel said, holding out her empty glass. Franny polished hers off, took Ethel's, and headed to the bar. I was a little worried that they would both pass out before I got any information out of Ethel, but her lips certainly were loosed.

When Franny turned back to me, I gave her what I hoped was a meaningful, even urgent, look. As she handed Ethel her refill, she asked, "By the way, dear, where *is* the money coming from to buy all those lovely clothes."

"Oh, now I'm 'dear', am I? You two must think I'm pretty goddamn stupid. Liquor me up a little and I'll spill the beans. Well, sorry, Ethel Dunn is one smart cookie!" She took an enormous swallow, puffed herself up into a Queen Elizabeth pose, and added with great nonchalance, "My affluence comes from my brother Charles."

"Who's he getting it from?"

"As if you didn't know."

"Vince Hammer?" I said.

"Oh goodness, someone went to college."

"How much does he give him?"

"Charles's retainer was in the six figures and there's been a recent bonus related to certain occurrences."

"You mean allowing Daphne Livingston's body to be cremated."

"I'm not at liberty to divulge that information."

"Does your brother think Daphne was murdered?"

"He's of two minds—probably and definitely."

"And who does he think did it?"

"Godfrey, of course."

"Really?" I said.

"No, I just said it to throw you off balance. Get a life, sister."

"That's not a bad idea," I said, standing up. "Franny, I'll call you about the antiques next week."

"What antiques?"

"This bourbon is quite pleasant," Ethel said.

"It's goddamn good!" Franny said.

"How does the wig look?" Ethel asked her.

"It's a becoming color," Franny said.

"I rather thought so."

"What should we have for dinner?"

"Let's call in for pizza," Ethel said.

"Smashing idea," Franny said.

As I left, they were pouring more bourbon and discussing toppings.

THIRTY-EIGHT

I HEADED DOWN RIVER Road on my way to the Rhinebeck police station to talk to Charlie Dunn. Armed with Ethel's bourbon-fueled admissions, I thought I might be able to pry some information out of him. Then I remembered it was Wednesday and that the blood Livingstons were meeting with Vince at his lawyer's office up in the Albany. It couldn't hurt to take one more look around Daphne's place.

I turned down the drive and drove through the decrepitude that was Westward Farm—rusting machinery, crumbling outbuildings, overgrown fields. The ruined romance of the place was starting to grow on me. I parked in high weeds behind an old garage uphill from the house, so I could sneak out unseen if I had to. The afternoon had grown more muggy, the sky hazier. Summer was settling in. And summer in the valley brought consuming heat and humidity, transforming the northern landscape into something close to southern gothic, a jungle of green vines and lazy animals, a slow-motion dance, full of languid longing and name-less lurking sorrow.

I headed down through the garden to the summerhouse. I stepped inside and looked around. Nothing had been touched, it was the same—an eccentric folly that had been allowed to slide into Gray Gardens decay. But there was something intangible in the air that I hadn't noticed before and I was struck by a memory…

When I was twelve, the boozy, defeated, put-upon aunt I was living with out on Long Island cribbed together enough money to send me to this ratty camp somewhere in the Poconos for two weeks. I'd say it was a sweet gesture, but she just wanted me out of the house so she could drink in peace. The camp was full of other screwed-up, farmed-out kids with no interest in archery, braiding lariats, or singing lame-ass songs (though we all dug gorging on the 'smores—especially after sucking down a doobie). The main activity at the place was sex—the counselors all fucked like bun-nies, and we ragingly hormonal campers cared only about making out, heavy petting, going *thisclose* to all the way, and then compar-ing detailed notes on same. The greatest challenge at camp, aside from winning the sack race, was finding safe secretive places for all this hanky-panky. Over the years several tryst spots had obtained near-mystical status, as in "I squeezed Johnny's dick under the kitchen" (the rickety wooden buildings were all built on lattice-covered platforms, providing commodious crawl spaces easily ac-cessed by horny adolescents) or "Linda let Ricky lick her *down there* out at the pine tree" or "Judy went down on Phil in the dead cabin." The dead cabin was an abandoned, collapsing hut reached by a serpentine trail through the woods. Summers of teenage bod-ies writhing, squeezing, and licking had left it littered with cigarette butts, beer cans, used condoms, and with a peculiar pungent smell, a mix of sweat and lust and loss.

Looking around the summerhouse where Daphne had died, I realized it reminded me of the dead cabin. There was a hint of that smell, pulled out of the old wood by the humidity. This was an abandoned place, too, one that had been adopted by Daphne to fulfill *her* secret lusts.

I sat on the flimsy wicker chair and looked out at the river. It was wide and slow and green; on the far bank Sawyerville spilled gently up the hill. I imagined Daphne out here, getting high, looking out at a view that was imprinted on her subconscious—one of the first things she had ever seen, and the last. I thought of her long wild life, of her sympathy and yearning, of the way she had sipped her wine and run her fingertip along the rim of the New Orleans glass.

I got up and began another search of the summerhouse, poring through the piles of leaves and mouse droppings, turning over the wicker furniture. Nothing. I stepped outside and began a widening concentric search of the surrounding lawn. I was on my third circle when I spotted something small and gray and cylindrical. I knelt down—a hypodermic needle. I gingerly picked it up, wrapped it in tissue, and slipped it into a plastic sandwich bag.

I headed up to the house. Downstairs, everything looked the same. Up in Daphne's bedroom someone had finally taken away the toast and tea, but otherwise things looked untouched. The room was starting to smell ripe—old clothes, old wine, old sweat, and that faint swampy whiff. I began one more methodical search. I opened all her dresser drawers, poked through her lingerie, scarves, sweaters. I cased the closet and bathroom, opening boxes and cabinets. I looked under the furniture and in the desk. Everything was ancient, from exclusive stores, of the highest quality, had a dreamy patina. It was a living museum of a fallen aristocrat.

I knelt down and slid my hand under the mattress. I hit something. I stood up and pulled up one side of the mattress, revealing a stash of photographs. I scooped them up and dropped the mattress. I sat on the edge of the bed and examined the photos.

They were taken with one of those old Polaroids. They were all of Daphne. All black and white. All recent. All riveting.

They showed her in black hose, garter belt, thong panties, bra, heels. Old flesh, fresh lust. There she was leaning over the vanity chair, ass out; standing legs spread with her fists on her hips; sitting wide in the chair with one foot up on the desk. In other shots she was wearing less and less, the poses more and more provocative. In each of them she was staring right into the camera, by turns defiant, seductive, dominant, submissive—but always looking out from another world, an outcast from this one, brave and lost and determined to grab onto some essence of life, sensation, feeling.

I was almost at the bottom of the stack when I came to the pictures taken out in the summerhouse.

THIRTY-NINE

OKAY, SO DAPHNE WAS still getting it on—quite spectacularly—at age seventy-something. Good for her. A lot of women have it happening well into old age. I had a client named Sadie who was in her eighties and picked up men at senior-citizen centers all over Brooklyn. The question here was: who took these pictures? And did he (or she) have something to do with Daphne's murder?

I pocketed the photos and headed downstairs. I walked into the parlor to find Maggie, with Rodent cradled on her naked hip, standing in front of an enormous portrait.

"See, baby girl, that's your great-grandma," Maggie was saying. The woman in the painting was imperious and patrician, standing beside the fireplace in this same parlor, looking out with a gaze that said, "Don't even *think* about messing with me."

"Hi," I said, trying to sound nonchalant.

"Howdy," Maggie said with a big goofy smile, seeming not at all surprised to see me. She had a huge joint dangling from her free hand. Say what you will about potheads, they *are* mellow. "I'm giving Rodent a tour of this side of the house."

Rodent had wide blue eyes, was pudgy and pinchable, and looked like she hadn't seen soap and water in weeks.

"So that's Daphne's mother?" I asked.

"Yeah, that's the old bitch," Maggie said, taking a deep suck on her joint. "She treated God like shit … By the way, who are you?"

"I'm Janet, we met a few weeks ago, I'm a friend of Daphne's."

"Oh … Daphne's dead."

"I know. I'm trying to find out how she died."

Maggie gave me a significant look. Then she put Rodent down. The tyke immediately ran into the middle of a priceless Oriental carpet, squatted down, and proudly peed. "I think she likes to mark her turf," Maggie confided. "Now, where were we?"

"We were talking about Daphne's death, how she died."

"She killed herself, she strung herself up from a beam down in the summerhouse." Maggie tilted her head and examined me for a second. "Shit, that's right! *You* found her."

"Yes."

"So why are you trying to figure out how she died?"

"I'm not sure she killed herself."

"You mean … somebody else killed her?"

I nodded.

"But isn't that murder?"

And the seasons, they go round and round …

"Do you remember that morning?" I asked.

"I don't remember *this* morning." She laughed and took another big toke. Rodent had climbed up into a priceless wing-backed chair and was bouncing up and down. I heard wood crack.

"'Course all my mornings are the same. Me and Godfrey make woo-woo."

"Okay."

"He says he can't work on his map without his morning muff." She laughed uproariously. In fact she couldn't stop laughing. Her flesh jiggled, every last roll. Rodent picked up a priceless figurine and flung it down to the floor, where it smashed into a million little pieces. She started laughing too, which only added to Maggie's merriment. Encouraged, Rodent smashed another priceless figurine. I just stood there, waiting for the hilarity to subside.

It took a while—and a few more figurines.

Maggie finally wound down, but she was left tuckered out, so she plotzed down to the floor, her legs splayed out in front of her. Rodent ran over and leapt into her arms.

"You know what, actually?" she said finally, looking up at me. "There was something weird that day ... at least I think it was that day ... after me and God were done, I was down in the kitchen cutting myself a slice of Entenmann's ... damn, I could use a slice of Entenmann's right now ... what's your favorite Entenmann's?"

"Raspberry cheese Danish."

"No, shit!! I fuckin' *love* raspberry cheese Danish." She looked at me like we'd just discovered we were long-lost sisters. "*Wow* ... we made a connection ... intense." Rodent was climbing up Maggie's body, using the fleshy crevices for toeholds.

"So you were saying about that day ... ?"

"What day?"

"The day Daphne died."

"Oh yeah. I looked out the kitchen window and I saw like *a man* come out of the woods and go into the summerhouse." Rodent had clambered onto Maggie's shoulders and her chubby hands were wrapped around her forehead.

"What did he look like?" I asked.

"What did who look like?"

"The man you saw go into the summerhouse."

"He looked like … a man."

"That's great, but was he white, black, Asian? Old, young? Tall, short, fat, thin, blond, bald, redhead?"

"*Whoa, sista!* You just asked like forty questions at one time," Maggie said, and then she giggled. "That's weird."

"I want ride, I want ride, I want ride!" Rodent chanted, grabbing hanks of Maggie's hair and pulling.

"Seriously, Maggie, can you remember anything about his looks?"

"I want ride, I want ride!"

"Just a second, Rodent, aunt Maggie is thinking … hmmm, let's see—he had legs and arms and a head …"

"What was he wearing?"

"He was wearing … clothes."

"What kind of clothes?"

"Shit, my joint went out, gotta light?"

"I want ride, I want ride!"

"Maggie, this is important, please try and remember something about what the man looked like."

She looked at me and opened her eyes wide. "This is heavy, isn't it?"

I nodded.

"Okay, I'd say he was … kinda young … yeah, kinda young … I think maybe he had a hat on so I couldn't see his face or tell for sure how old he was. "

"Gimme ride!!"

Maggie lumbered to her feet with Rodent on board.

"I gotta go find a light."

"You can't remember anything else?"

"I'm pretty sure he was solid, like muscles, and tall … but he might have been short."

"Giddyup!"

"Isn't she the cutest little tidbit?" Maggie said, trotting out of the room shouting, "Hold on there, pard'ner, hold on!"

FORTY

I PARKED IN FRONT of the Rhinebeck police station, next to a big fat Cadillac. I walked inside and up to the counter. No sign of life. Then I heard muffled grunting/moaning sounds from down the hall. I peeked my head around—Charlie Dunn's office door was closed and that's where the grunting/moaning was coming from.

Whatever.

I sat in one of the two plastic chairs and picked up a tattered copy of *Field and Stream*. There was a story about how all the gas and oil leases that had been granted under Bush were fucking up the hunting out west—land that used to belong to the people now belonged to a few people. It was nice to see all those hunters finally waking up to who their real enemies were.

The grunting/moaning swelled into a cacophony of agonized ecstasy—I'm not sure if I agree with Freud that every orgasm is a little death, but some of them sure sound like it.

After a minute or so I heard the door open and close, and then the world's oldest cheerleader sashayed around the counter. She was around forty, had major blonde hair, big tits, lots of makeup, and was wearing a skimpy cheerleading outfit and carrying a pom-pom.

"Hi," she said nonchalantly.

"Go team."

"You got that right," she said with a smile. Then she pulled a compact out of her purse, checked her makeup, reapplied her lipstick, took out one of those tiny packets of breath strips, placed one in her mouth, and walked out. Her card probably read: Have Tongue, Will Travel.

I walked up to the counter and said a loud, "Hello?"

After a minute, Charlie Dunn opened the door and headed toward me, still adjusting himself. A little smile played at the corners of his mouth. "What can I do for you?"

"What *have* you done for Vince Hammer is more like it," I said.

"I don't have time to play games."

"Recent events contradict that statement," I said, nodding toward his office. That little smile again. It was starting to work my nerves. "I just have one quick question."

"Shoot."

"Is it legal for a chief of police to accept a six-figure retainer from a real estate developer? We won't even mention the monthly fee and recent bonus."

My smile-eraser did its job.

"I don't know what you're talking about," he said, sweat breaking out on his upper lip.

"Yes, you do."

"I got work to do."

"I hope you got it in cash, because if there's any kind of paper trail, well, some folks frown on cops on the take. You don't look so good, Charlie. Was it something you ate?"

"I don't have to stand here and listen to this."

"Would you rather sit down and listen to it? Because you *will* listen. I want to know everything you know about Daphne Livingston's murder."

"I don't know anything."

"Bullshit."

He looked me square in the eye—I looked right back. He exhaled with a loud sigh.

"I have no goddamn idea who killed her, okay? And that's the truth."

"But you did compromise the crime scene, violate procedure by allowing her body to be cremated, and impede any possible investigation."

He made a resigned face, and scratched the back of his neck. "What do you want to know?"

"Did you have any advance warning of any kind?"

"No."

"No word from Vince Hammer or anyone else that something might be about to go down at Westward Farm?"

"I knew the situation there was . . . unsettled."

"How did you know that?"

"This is a small town, people talk. Everyone knew Daphne had come back home, and that she was in bad shape. Probably mixed up with drugs."

"Did you pass that information on to Vince Hammer?"

From his little flinch I knew I'd hit pay dirt.

"Look, Vince Hammer has been making himself known in these parts for years now," he said. "He donates to every charity from Westchester to Albany. He gets around, gets to know people who might be useful. We had an officer who was hit by a drunk driver two years ago, poor guy was paralyzed. Hammer contributed a lot of money to his medical fund. He knows how to make friends. One day he asked me out to lunch. Kept bringing up Westward Farm. Wanted to know everything about the Livingstons. I mean *everything*."

"So the two of you established channels of communication."

"You might say that."

"I just did. And what exactly did you know about Daphne's drug use?"

"Look, we have a lot less of a drug problem over here than they do across the river. I heard that she got her drugs from a woman over there, that they were delivered by boat, by that Pillow woman."

"And you never took any action?"

He exhaled again and just stood there, waiting me out.

"I guess I'd call that malignant neglect," I said. "Did you hear anything about Daphne having a lover?"

He snorted a laugh. "Now that's a pretty picture."

"You're one to talk."

"I think I'm done talking."

He turned and walked back to his office.

FORTY-ONE

I CALLED DETECTIVE CHEVRONA Williams and told her I wanted to see her. She asked me to come down to the State Police barracks on Route 209 south of Kingston. I drove across the river and headed down 209. The building was squat and unimpressive. I was directed to the detective's small cluttered office. She looked tired and sad. But she still looked good.

"Cup of undrinkable coffee?" she said as I took my seat.

"With that recommendation, I'll pass."

"What have you got?"

I filled her in on what I'd learned from Ethel, Maggie, and Charlie.

"Very interesting," she said. "We have to find that man Maggie saw. Unless she was hallucinating, I think that information means we can pretty much rule out Godfrey, in spite of the cigarette butt."

"I think you're right."

I took out the hypodermic and handed it to her.

"I'll send this to the lab and ask for an expedited analysis."

"Doesn't this all add up to some serious resources being put into this case?" I asked.

"Unfortunately, no. I've talked to my superiors, and they won't budge. This is one of those cases they just want to go away. Allowing Daphne's body to be cremated was a real mistake, and they're embarrassed by that. Then there's all Vince Hammer's pressure to let this sleeping dog lie. I'd have to say the fix is in."

"I think I will take that cup of coffee," I said.

Chevrona stood up. "In for a dime, in for a donut?"

"Why not."

While she went to get my coffee, I let it sink in: If Daphne's murder was going to be solved, it was going to be solved by me. My fascination with murder—with *the ability* to murder, with the dark festering heart—was growing obsessive. I'd never worked with hardcore criminals in my practice, but I had seen ambition, greed, and rage so extreme that they overpowered conscience and reason and led people into dangerous behaviors. I ran everything I'd seen and heard over in my mind, hoping for some pattern to emerge, for one single piece of evidence to leap out. This was definitely a well-planned, well-executed crime. I searched for the one person possessed enough to take the cosmic leap from wishing Daphne were dead to actually killing her. I was now positive that Esmerelda had given me a clue that dawn back at the Lighthouse. What was it she had said... "Pale horse, pale rider, dark horse, dead rider... if you don't pay the piper, the piper won't play... but the piper will sing."

Chevrona came back with my coffee and a pink-frosted donut. What a flirt.

"I know where your mind is going right now, Janet. But remember: to convict someone of murder you need a lot more than circumstantial evidence. Especially when you've got powerful forces aligned against you."

"I made one other interesting discovery."

I took out the stack of photographs and handed them to her. She flipped through them, betraying no emotion. "Interesting. Daphne had it going on. But whether this connects to her death is another story." She leaned forward on her desk. "Be careful, be very careful."

We sat there in silence for a moment.

"You look a little tried," I said.

"I am tired."

"Work?" I asked.

Detective Williams looked at me for a moment, trying to decide whether to open up or not. I put on my best sympathetic-therapist face.

"Yeah, work." She hesitated, looked down. I'd seen that look so many times in my practice. She wanted to talk, needed to talk. But it's tough. I knew it was best to let it ride. It rode … until finally: "And home. Things suck at home …"

She stopped herself, fought to hold down the words.

"I'm a former therapist," I said.

"No shit."

I nodded. We sat there in silence again.

"How about I buy you a drink?" I said.

"That's the best offer I've had in awhile."

FORTY-TWO

WE DROVE UP TO the Rondout, a hip Kingston neighborhood hard by the Rondout Creek where it flows into the Hudson. This was one end of the old Delaware and Hudson Canal, which opened in 1826 and linked the two rivers. For a brief period in the late nineteenth century this corner of Kingston was one of the most prosperous places in the state. It's filled with cool old architecture, bars, restaurants, galleries, a marina. I liked it down there, it had character and there were enough people around to make it feel urban. Chevrona and I went into a little French bistro, sat at a small table by the bar. She ordered a beer, I ordered a glass of red wine.

"It's nice around here," she said.

"Where do you live?"

"Way the hell out in the country, Margaretsville."

"You like it?"

"I did."

She downed her beer and signaled to the bartender for another. She wasn't quite ready to spill.

"I'm still working on the Pillow case," she said, changing the subject.

"Who do you think killed her?"

"My bet is still that it was a rival drug dealer, maybe from up in Albany. This is a decent-sized market and with her gone, it's wide open. And the way she was murdered, it was overkill, designed to send a message: this is my turf now."

"Do you have any evidence?"

"Well, we've asked around on the street in Newburgh and Albany, and everyone seems to know she's dead. But no one's talking about who might be responsible. But we're going to wait for things to die down and then see who moves in on her territory."

"What about that guy I saw pick her up in his boat that morning?"

"Morris Emmett, out of Albany, guy has his finger in a thousand pies, all of them rancid. But we can't touch him, he's way too smart." She finished her second beer, signaled for a third. Then she turned to me, suddenly looking completely miserable, and said in a quiet voice, "My partner decided she's not gay anymore."

My first thought: that partner is an idiot.

We just sat for a while. Gotta sit sometimes. "How long have you two been together?" I asked finally.

"Six years."

"And out of the blue she told you she's not gay anymore?"

"She started sleeping with some guy." Her face got hard. Then her eyes filled with tears. "Shit," she muttered under her breath, fighting them down. Her beer came and she drank half of it in one swallow. "You should know something about me: I do *not* cry."

"I didn't see a thing."

"Yeah, he owns a garage up in Delhi, and Lucy took her car in for a tune-up. She got a tune-up alright. That motherfucker. And I thought she was it, ever-and-ever time."

"No such thing."

"No such fucking thing. The worst part is going back there every night. Place feels like a meat locker."

"How long has she been seeing this guy?"

"About a month."

"Do you think it's serious or just a fling?"

"I honestly don't know. I'm sleeping in the den and we don't talk much." Chevrona pushed her chair back from the table, put her hands on her knees, took several deep breaths. "What do you think I should do?"

I got a charge that she trusted me enough to ask me that question. "I think you should be talking with Lucy. You have six years together and whatever happens, you owe each other consideration."

"Talking about this shit doesn't come easy to me."

"There aren't a lot of people it *does* come easy to. But if you two start talking, at least you'll be able to figure out where you stand. Then you'll be able to think about your next move."

She polished off her beer. "Thanks," she said.

I shrugged.

"This is going to sound weird," she said, "but I'm glad I've got Pillow's murder to work on. Murder is murder, but love is ..." She searched for the words—but then let out a soul-deep sigh.

I'd never heard it put better.

FORTY-THREE

Josie put the scrambled eggs down in front of me. Sputnik sat next to me, waiting for his taste.

"They're not as good as Abba's, but ..." she said. Then she went back to the kitchen and busied herself cleaning up, head down, pretending not to be waiting for my reaction. The haircut she'd gotten from George and Abba was a big improvement, framing her face in a way that brought out her large, soulful brown eyes. They'd also been buying her clothes, cool stuff that fit well and made her look smart and fresh.

I took a bite—Josie had grated in some romano and chopped up some dandelion greens she'd "harvested" from my mostly concrete backyard and tossed them in, giving the eggs a tasty tang.

"They're delicious," I said.

Josie looked up at me, trying to keep a lid on her beam.

"Aren't you going to join me?" I asked.

She brought her plate over and sat across from me at the round oak table.

"So, how's it going down in Kingston?" I asked.

"Good."

"More, please."

She took a bite of her own eggs and sadness swept across her face. But she pushed it away. "It's hard to find me a foster family. Because of my age."

"What if they can't find you one?"

"Don't worry, I'll leave."

"I just asked a question."

"There are group homes. There is one in Albany my social worker thinks she can get me into."

"All right."

"But she'd like to keep trying to find me a better situation. Once I go into the group home she says it will be impossible to find a foster family."

We ate in silence for a while. No matter how many bites I took, my plate kept getting fuller. Yes, Josie was a good kid who deserved a chance. Yes, Josie was no trouble. Yes, I had an extra room. Yes-yes-yes... *NO!*

I left a few bites of egg on my plate and put it down on the floor for Sputnik, who inhaled it. "You have another fan of your cooking."

"He'll eat anything," Josie said.

"This is true."

"I'm getting pretty good on the computer," she said. "Do you know you have wifi here?"

"No kidding."

"It must be from a neighbor. I got online last night."

"Great."

I hate the Internet. When it first came out I was like: oh, wow, cool, fun, I can access anything—now it's just a black hole, an energy suck, a vomitorium of information, a headache with a keyboard attached.

"Have you thought of selling on eBay?" Josie asked.

"I've *thought* of it, but it's a lot of work."

"Would you like me to try selling something?"

I picked up the plate from the floor and took it over to the sink. Then I turned to her. "Josie, this is my business, my home, my life ... I just, um, how can I say this? I was married to a bastard who left me after ten years and it really did a number to my head ... and my heart. I'm just pulling myself back together, and I feel like I have to be a little selfish right now. Does that make any sense?"

"It makes sense."

"Thanks," I said.

"It also makes sense for you to let me try to sell something on eBay. I'm not asking you to adopt me."

I looked at her in surprise. She met my gaze—and there was a feisty gleam in her eye. You know, there's nothing in this whole goddamn motherfucking shit pile of a world more beautiful than seeing a feisty gleam come into the eye of a kid like Josie.

"All right, kiddo, you're on," I said, turning back to the sink and washing my plate. "Just find anything that looks promising and give it a whirl."

Josie ran into her room and was back in a flash with two rubber squeeze toys from the 1950s—a towheaded boy and girl, sort of a three-dimensional *Fun with Dick and Jane.*

"What about these two?" she asked.

"They're pretty adorable," I said.

"Kinda creepy, too."

"I can see that."

"Should I set a reserve?"

"Wait a minute, this is your thing."

She nodded. "Okay." Then she disappeared back into her room.

I thought for a moment and then called out to her, "Listen, while you're online, see if you can find out anything about a Marcella Sedgwick."

"Spell it," Josie called back.

FORTY-FOUR

OLANA IS AN OPIUM-PIPE dream, a Moorish castle that sits on a hill high above the east bank of the Hudson. It was built by the landscape painter Frederic Edwin Church in the 1870s, inspired by his travels to the Middle East. The exterior is all exotic tile and brickwork capped by a minaret. Inside, it's an enfolding harem of Oriental carpets and velvet drapes, dark, moody, dramatic. I parked in the lot and walked to the front of the house. I looked out at the sweeping southern view—Church had put in a heart-shaped pond that glittered in the foreground, framed by the river and valley beyond. It was a windy day with skittering clouds, and the air smelled like the past, leafy and sad. Church thought the Hudson Valley was the most blessed place on earth, the center of the artistic and spiritual world. Standing there, it was easy to believe.

I spotted Claire on the lawn, sitting on a plaid blanket with a picnic basket by her side. She was wearing well-cut khakis, a blue blouse, and chic sandals. With her legs tucked under her, her hair combed behind her ears, her face clean and fresh, she looked like

Nantucket, summer benefits at country museums, ease, grace, entitlement. She saw me and waved. I headed over.

"Isn't this heavenly?" she asked, indicating the view.

"It is," I said, sitting.

"I come here when I need to recharge. It's my refuge." She ran her fingers through her hair, chin tilted up—she was very pretty. "I brought us a little *je ne sais quoi*—just lemonade and cookies." She opened a bottle of fancy Italian lemonade and poured me a glass. Then she opened a tin filled with cookies. "I baked these myself."

"Really?"

"No," she said with a disarming smile, "but they're from a wonderful little place in Tivoli."

The lemonade was delicious and cookie scrumptious.

"First of all," Claire said, "I want to apologize for my behavior at Vince Hammer's. It was inexcusable."

"Apology accepted."

"As you may have noticed, there's a slight vein of rage that runs through my family," she said with a wry smile. "And being home has been *very* difficult for me. The scab just gets ripped off the wound, and you realize it hasn't really healed at all. But I've been doing lots of yoga and focusing on my work. I feel much better." She looked down, plucked at the grass. "I was fond of my Aunt Daphne. She was always kind and encouraging. She's the only one in the family who asked me about my job at Bard, who showed any pride in what I was doing." She looked up at me. "I'd like to help you find her murderer."

"I'd appreciate that. Is there anything you can tell me?"

"I know she met Esmerelda Pillow at a bar in Catskill. They became friends. Daphne was always attracted to people who were … if I were being kind I'd say eccentric; if I were being honest I'd say degenerate. Esmerelda would come to visit, by boat. They would sit in the summerhouse together. I thought they were drinking buddies. I didn't realize there were drugs involved. But it would explain Daphne's deterioration over the last few months."

"So you met Esmerelda?"

"A couple of times, yes. I found her very off-putting, bizarre and shifty. The drug connection helps me understand why Daphne tolerated her."

"Do you think it's possible she and Daphne were lovers?"

"Good God, what a thought."

I told her about the photographs.

"Trust Daphne to deliver a surprise, even from the grave." She smiled. "I don't think it was Esmerelda, though. I didn't sense anything like that."

"Can you think of anyone else it might be?"

"This is going to sound very sick—welcome to Livingston world—but I wouldn't be shocked if it was my father."

"Really? I thought they hated each other."

"They did, but it's a thin line. Daphne and Godfrey always had a *very* intense relationship—and he does own an old Polaroid." She sighed. "Just when you think it's safe to go back in the water. Do you think her lover, whoever it was, killed her?"

"I don't." I thought of telling Claire about the man who had appeared out of the woods, but thought better of it. "The pictures could be completely unrelated to her death."

"What I wanted to tell you was that about a week before she died, Daphne told me that she was going to be going away for a while. I asked her why. She was vague, but she mentioned Esmerelda. She seemed scared. I think Daphne got in a little too deep. That she was beginning to mistrust Esmerelda, to be afraid of her. Daphne was always very intuitive. I think she *sensed* something."

Just then a voice called, "Claire!"

We looked over—a young couple about Claire's age were approaching us. The woman was wearing an almost identical outfit to Claire, and the man was in jeans and a white oxford shirt with a thick brown-leather belt and matching flip-flops. They both radiated upper-class ease.

Claire leapt up.

"Boops!" she said, hugging the woman.

I'm sorry, but WASP nicknames are *weird*.

"How great to see you!" Boops gushed. Then she held Claire at arm's length and scrutinized her face, as if looking for cracks. "How *are* you?" she asked, a little too sincerely.

"I'm fine, just fine," Claire answered, a little too casually.

"I heard a rumor you were back. You haven't called."

"I've been so busy," Claire said. "I'm teaching at Bard."

"How fan*tas*tic! You really are okay." There was an awkward silence and then Boops said, "Oh, I'm sorry, this is Mark Warren, my fiancé."

"How do you do?" Claire said.

"What a pleasure," Mark said, and they shook hands.

There was another awkward pause, and then Claire turned to me. "And this is Janet Petrocelli."

I could see Boops take me in—and peg me as N.O.C.D. (Not Our Class, Dear)—but she turned on a warm smile and handshake. "How nice to meet you," she said.

I nodded to them both.

The wind gusted. Claire crossed her shins, her shoulders went up. "So … when's the big day?" she asked with a strained smile.

"September. You must come," Boops said.

"I will."

"I heard about Daphne. I'm sorry," Boops said. "Of course, none of us had seen her in years."

"She was a fascinating woman," Claire said, straightening up.

"Yes … she certainly had quite a life … well …" Boops slipped her arm through Mark's. "Mark is from Santa Barbara and he's never seen Olana."

"You're in for a treat," Claire said.

Boops kissed Claire on the cheek. "We'll get together."

"Okay."

"I'm really happy that you're … teaching. Call me." As she and Mark walked away she leaned into him and said something.

Claire sat back down.

"Old friend?" I asked.

"She's an Alcott," Claire said, as if that explained everything. She took several deep breaths. "'I'm really happy that you're … *teaching*.' What she meant was: 'I'm really surprised you're not in a straightjacket.' You see, I had a little … *break* when I was fifteen. I spent a few months at the Center for Living in Hartford. I have fought my way back tooth and nail to my current state of semi-sanity. Fuck you, Boops. *Fuck you*." Her eyes filled with tears.

It really was a curse, having my so-called sympathetic face. There's a saying in dentistry: "Drill, fill, send 'em the bill." One of my former colleagues amended it to: "Sit still, let 'em spill, send 'em the bill."

194

The only problem was I was no longer sending anyone a bill.

Claire made a big effort to pull herself together. "I'm sorry, I—"

"It's okay," I said.

"I've never had a relationship that lasted more than one date."

"I'm sorry about that, but ..."

"I'm frigid. I loathe sex, I loathe being touched, I loathe men."

"Claire ..."

"Do you blame me? You've met my father."

"I can imagine that it was very difficult."

"Look." She held out her wrists and I saw the scars.

"Claire, I think you should be talking to a therapist."

"Why, are you worried that I'll kill myself?" The tears were streaming down her face now. She closed her eyes and took in an enormous breath. Then she reached into the picnic basket, took out a tissue, and blew her nose. "You'll have to forgive me, *again.*"

"Of course."

"I'm really fine. I'm going to get a dog. A rescue dog. I'll be back home in a couple of months. I've got a dissertation to finish."

"What's the subject?"

"American pastoral: Eden or illusion?" She looked out at the view. "Aunt Daphne was the first person to bring me here. I think I was six. We toured the house. She knew everything about Church, his art, his life. I can still remember her passion that afternoon. She came alive, and of course she looked divine in those days. People noticed her. Then we came out here and sat on this lawn, very close to this very spot, on a blanket a lot like this one. She had brought a bottle of wine for herself and a can of Coke for me, which was thrilling—Coke was verboten at home. At one point she took my face in her hands and told me I was going to have a special life, a wonderful life."

Claire looked down at her lap, smoothed out her khakis. Then she turned to me with a warm smile, and asked, "Can I interest you in another cookie?"

FORTY-FIVE

"Look," George said, holding out his hand as I climbed into his hearse. A huge silver, turquoise, and onyx ring sat there on his left ring finger. "Dwayne and I exchanged rings."

"It's big," I said.

"Our love is big."

"Have you met his wife yet?"

"I love his wife. There's absolutely no animosity. My relationship with Dwayne is wide and pliant, forgiving, yielding. There's room in it for all three of us."

"In other words, nothing has changed."

"Janet, for the sake of our continued friendship, I think we should agree not to discuss Dwayne."

"All right."

"But don't you see how unfair not discussing him is to me, he's the center of my life right now."

"You're the one who suggested we not discuss him."

"You were supposed to contradict me. Not discussing him is a complete denial of my inner truth."

"Okay, okay, let's discuss him."

"Now I don't want to, you've ruined it."

Thankfully, we arrived at our destination—the lighthouse parking lot. We got out of the car and started down the trail. It was early evening and the light was soft. Summer had settled over the valley, but at this hour the heat was soft, too.

After a little way we left the trail and moved through the underbrush toward Mad John's pad. George let out a birdcall to let him know we were approaching. The reeds parted and Mad John's face appeared.

"Hey, people, how's it hanging?" he asked, grinning like a Jack-o'-lantern.

We stepped through the reeds into Mad John's abode.

"Place looks great," George said.

Mad John had tarted things up with two battered folding lawn chairs, a life-size cardboard Jackie Chan movie display, and a defunct computer monitor covered with the kind of glittery horse and star stick-ums that pre-adolescent girls put on everything. In one corner there was a sculptural pile of junk that looked like it had been scavenged from behind a Radio Shack: a jumble of dead computers, DVD players, cameras, telephones.

"I'm into décor," Mad John said.

"So, we're going to take a little raft trip," George said.

The only way to get to Esmerelda Pillow's house by land was to drive down a narrow peninsula that jutted out into the Hudson, past a half dozen neighbors. We wanted to reconnoiter without anyone knowing it.

Mad John did his jumping-up-and-down-in place thing. "Goin' out on the river, goin' out, yah-yah!!"

We followed him through the reeds to the riverbank. It was almost twilight in the gnarly inlet, Mad John's watery dream world, and the river glowed and glittered and civilization seemed a million miles away.

We climbed on the raft, Mad John untied and pushed us off. We headed out from the bank and then he turned south. The little red running lights of boats moved up and down the river.

"Isn't this heavenly?" George said.

"River magic, moving and flowing, never stopping," Mad John said. Then he started singing—gibberish, but mournful gibberish, in a strangely beautiful voice. On shore lights came on in the houses, cozy and twinkly. For a moment I could forget about Daphne's murder and all the possible scenarios that were racing around in my head. The warm languid evening felt like it would never end, the gentle lolling of the raft cradled me and I was suffused with a sense of freedom and adventure. This was what I had moved upstate for—a different life, a chance to slip out of the ordinary, to feel wonder and wondrous again.

"I wish Dwayne were here," George sighed. "He's a hopeless romantic."

"Dwayne is stupy-woopy," Mad John said with a cackle.

"You know, Mad John, I always thought you were a sensitive guy, but that is a totally shallow thing to say. There are a lot of different kinds of intelligence. Dwayne is intuitive, he can look at me and tell what I'm feeling."

"Yeah—*horny!*" Mad John crowed. "He stupy-woopy!"

"Mad John, Dwayne is an orphan, he had a traumatic childhood that included neglect, abuse, trauma, addiction, jail, parole, recidivism. He's deeply wounded."

"He's also stupy-woopy."

"I give up, it's impossible to have a rational discussion with you!"

"Well, *duh*."

We reached the skinny peninsula, at the end of which sat Esmerelda Pillow's ramshackle house. Mad John deftly guided the raft ashore, past the half-submerged supermarket cart. He beached on the edge of the ratty, trash-strewn lawn and we all disembarked. It was dark, quiet, and creepy out here.

The three of us walked silently toward the house. It was clad in dented, buckling aluminum siding. There was a glassed-in porch facing the river. All the blinds were drawn. We went around the side. The door was unlocked. We stepped inside the porch, which opened to the living room.

I took out my flashlight and flipped it on—the batteries were dead.

"Shit, Nancy Drew forgot to check her fucking batteries," said George

"Oh, let's just turn on a light, who cares?" Mad John said.

"What if someone sees it?" I asked.

"We'll flee by sea," Mad John said.

"Anyhow, the nearest neighbor is up the road a ways and there are a lot of trees," George said.

Mad John found a switch and flipped it.

Wow!

Esmerelda's place may have looked like Tobacco Road from the outside, but the inside was strictly Easy Street—joint looked like a spread in *Metropolitan Home*, all mid-century furniture highlighted with geometric rugs, perfect finishes, bold art, trendy tchotchkes.

Mad John leapt up on one of the couches and started jumping up and down, chanting, "Groovy pad, groovy pad, groovy pad!" It was very Rodent of him.

We walked through the living room and into the kitchen, which looked like the contractors had left ten minutes ago—stainless-steel countertops, cherrywood cabinets, red enamel appliances, with not a morsel of food in sight. The master bedroom was a glamorous cocoon, with wall-to-wall beige carpet and a low-slung bed. Mad John fell to the floor and started to roll around like a dog. Tactile little guy.

The bathroom was marble, with a steam shower and whirlpool tub.

"Well, now we know where all her drug profits went," George said as we stood admiring the stainless steel bidet.

"She was living out some aging-rock-star fantasy," I said. "It's really bizarre, the way she left the outside all rundown."

"And brilliant," George said. "That way, her taxes don't go up. And people don't start asking a lot of questions about where her dough comes from."

We cased the house quickly and silently while Mad John bounced, rolled, sniffed, and humped everything in sight. The place was organized down to the toothpick and we found her stash of pot in the kitchen—a slide-out refrigerator drawer filled with a half-dozen bricks of the stuff.

"Tempting," George said, eyeing the bounty. Then he resolutely closed the drawer, announcing, "No way, Dwayne is clean and sober."

"Is that court-ordered?"

"Who told you?" George got a faraway look in his eye. "What an amazing man. To have lived through four years at Elmira State and still have the faith and courage to love another man."

"It may be a habit he picked up *at* Elmira State."

"You know, somewhere in New York City there's probably a recovery group for former clients of Janet Petrocelli."

"That's a recurring nightmare of mine."

Under the marijuana drawer was a flat cherrywood panel. When I pushed it, it sprung open, revealing a hidden drawer secured with three padlocks.

"That must be where the hard drugs are," George said.

I rattled the locks—they were serious.

"We need a metal saw to get those suckers off," George said.

"I'll have to come back."

In the far corner of one of the kitchen counters I noticed a phone answering machine. It was a bit of an anachronism in this day of voice mail, but I could relate—I still used one. And, unlike cell phones, there was no easily accessible record of who has been calling you or of your own location, security features a drug dealer might prize. The number three was illuminated in the calls received box. I pressed play. The first two calls were hang-ups, then:

"It's me. Got it. Will deliver."

I'd recognize that monosyllabic eloquence anywhere.

FORTY-SIX

Josie put down the plates of enchiladas, rice, beans, and guacamole in front of George and me.

"You made these from scratch?" I asked.

Josie nodded.

"*Mmmmmmmm!*" George moaned after his first bite. "These are the best enchiladas ever in the history of the planet."

"George is so understated," Josie said with a big smile.

"So are you—I had no idea you could cook like this," I said, savoring the spicy mix of chicken and vegetables.

"Neither did I," Josie admitted. She sat down with her own plate. "I found out a few things about Marcella Sedgwick online."

"Tell all," I said.

"Well, she has three degrees, from Yale, Penn, and UCLA."

"Anything else?"

"Yes, this is interesting. She's originally from Elkton, Kentucky, a small town in the southwest corner of the state."

"I thought she was from an old East Coast family," I said.

"According to Todd County court documents I found, she had her name legally changed when she was fifteen years old. Her real name is Amber Lundy. Her mother's age at the time was twenty-eight, and her father's address was 'whereabouts unknown.'"

I put down my fork.

"Is the food okay?" Josie asked.

I nodded. Just then my cell phone rang.

"Chevrona Williams here. I just got the lab analysis back on the contents of the hypodermic needle. Heroin and recuronium."

"Recuronium?" I asked.

George perked up.

"It's a paralytic agent," Chevrona said. "It's not a fun way to die. Your body freezes, but you're still fully aware."

"That would explain the expression on Daphne's face when I found her."

"Her last moments were hell."

"I think this proves that Esmerelda wasn't acting alone," I said. "Were there any fingerprints on the hypodermic?"

"No."

"Do you think the powers-that-be will show more interest in the case now?"

"No, but it gives me a little leeway to keep pursuing it on my own," she said.

"Thanks for the info."

"Stay in close touch, Janet."

I hung up.

"Recuronium, huh?" George said.

"How do you get hold of it?" I asked.

"A hospital would be a good place to start. It's used as an anesthetic in most surgeries."

I put my hand on George's arm. "I need your help."

FORTY-SEVEN

BENEDICTINE HOSPITAL IS IN midtown Kingston, on a hill a few blocks south of Broadway. It's a sprawling complex of mismatched red brick buildings, added over the years. George, wearing his surgical scrubs, parked his hearse in the lot.

"Just follow my lead," he said as we crossed the lot.

The inside looked like every other hospital I'd ever been in—florescent-lit corridors, lots of signage, donor plaques, banks of elevators, everything rose colored, made of molded plastic. Founded by nuns, Benedictine had the requisite Jesuses and soothing biblical quotes sprinkled around—but discreetly, thank God.

"Poor Dwayne was in here for three weeks last year," George said.

"What happened?"

"He fell off the roof of his van and broke his tailbone."

"What was he doing on the roof of his van?"

"He doesn't remember."

"Hi, George," a maintenance worker said as we passed. There were other waves, smiles, hellos.

"They love me here," George said. We turned a corner. "Okay, straight ahead on our right you'll see the pharmacy. That's where the surgical trays come from—they have sterilized instruments, bandages and packing, and, of course, the anesthetics."

I followed him past the pharmacy, around another corner, and into the surgical ward. There was a circular counter in the center of the main reception, manned by a nurse—a skinny woman in her thirties, mixed race, with spiky hair and something like forty thin silver bracelets on one forearm. In my experience, nurses tend to be pretty cool people.

"Well, look what the cat dragged in," she said.

"Hey, Wanda, how's it hanging?"

"They're *not* hanging, same as usual," she said, looking down at her flat chest. "How are *yours* hanging?"

George mock-cupped his balls, "Loose and low."

They laughed.

"Busy day?" George asked.

"Kinda slow. Two hip replacements and a valve repair. Are you here to work, I didn't see you on the schedule?"

"I may put in a shift in the ER, someone called in sick," George said vaguely. "But right now I'm showing my pal Janet around. She's new to the area and is thinking of volunteering here."

"We could use you," Wanda said.

"What do volunteers do in the surgical wing?" I asked.

"If we have an emergency, like a car crash, it's all hands on deck in the operating room, so we need people out here at the desk. And on regular days it's good to have a civilian around for the families while they wait out the operations, helps with their anxiety. Volunteers also run general errands, like bringing the surgical trays over from the pharmacy."

"How does that work?" I asked, leaning on the counter.

"You go to the pharmacy and ask for Dr. So-and-so's tray, and wheel it over here."

"I could probably handle that."

"If you try really hard," George said. "Listen, Wanda, do you know who the developer Vince Hammer is?"

"I don't live under a rock."

"Doesn't his girlfriend Marcella Sedgwick volunteer here?"

Wanda rolled her eyes. "Queen'cella we call her. She waltzes in here dressed for the red carpet. And she always brings a little wicker basket full of cookies and fancy little sandwiches. It's very noblesse oblige, but they are tasty."

"Does she get her hands dirty?"

"Not if she can help it," Wanda said. "She loves to flirt with the surgeons, so her favorite job is retrieving the surgical cart."

"Thanks, Wanda. George, can you show me the rest of the hospital now," I asked, already on my way out.

FORTY-EIGHT

AN HOUR LATER, I rang the intercom at Vince Hammer's estate.

"Yes?" came the disembodied lackey's reply.

"Janet Petrocelli here to see Vince and Marcella."

"Are they expecting you?"

"Yes," I lied.

The gate swung open. I drove up and parked. I hustled up the front steps and the doors opened just as I reached the top. I hoped to find Marcus, but it was a clean-cut clone. He ushered me in.

In the living room I saw Vince and a small crowd gathered around a large table.

"Janet, come join us," he called to me in a we're-best-friends voice.

As I got closer I saw that the table held a scale model of a large development that looked a lot like River Landing.

"This is a friend of mine, Janet Petrocelli. These are my architects. As soon as Marcella comes down they're going to make a full presentation," Vince said.

I smiled at the assembled crew, who looked bright and proud.

"These people are brilliant, Janet. They moved all the buildings a thousand feet from the nearest newt habitat. We've reduced the height of the towers by eight stories. And we've added a theater and cultural center to give River Landing that extra cachet. Nothing moves the approval process along faster than a little culture."

I looked at the model. It would have looked great with a toy train running through it. Sitting next to the Hudson it would be a disaster.

"Vince, I need to talk to you alone a minute," I said.

A Tony Soprano look flashed across his face. Then he smiled.

"Of course. I'll be right back," he said to the crew.

Vince led me to a corner of the dining room, "What's up?"

I took out my cell phone and played Marcus's message to Esmerelda for him.

"That came off of Esmerelda Pillow's answering machine," I said.

"I don't understand what this has to do with me."

"I think you do."

"Look, I don't make trouble, I don't need trouble. I'm going to own this valley. Do you really think I'd risk it all to knock off some old lush who would be dead in a few years anyway?"

Just then Marcella appeared, looking gorgeous, glowing, but just a bit disheveled.

When she saw me, she said, "What's she doing here?"

"Being a pain in the ass."

Marcella narrowed her eyes and looked at me. Then, like a switch, she gave me a big warm smile, followed by an air kiss on each cheek.

"Janet, why don't you come listen to the presentation? We're going to serve champagne and lobster rolls. I'm president of the new cultural center, we want to be on par with Dia Beacon and the Gehry at Bard. It's all terribly exciting and we'd love to have you onboard—it's going to turn Sawyerville into a world-class destination."

"Is Marcus around?"

Something flashed through Marcella's eyes but it was gone before I could figure out exactly what it was. But I had an inkling.

"I think he's somewhere. Have you seen him, Vince?"

"Okay, this meeting is over," Vince announced.

"I'm not leaving until I talk to Marcus."

"I could have you thrown out," Vince said.

"Oh, darling, don't be silly. Why don't you let me handle Janet?"

"She's all yours," Vince said, walking away.

"Now, what's this all about?" Marcella asked.

"It's about the murders of Daphne Livingston and Esmerelda Pillow, Amber."

She went dead still—for just a nanosecond. Then she tossed her hair and said, "Marcella suits me much better, don't you think?"

"Amber by any other name."

"Vince knows all about my background, in fact he respects me far more than if I were to the manor born."

"Does he know that a hypodermic discovered near Daphne's body contained traces of recuronium?"

This time it took her slightly more than a nanosecond to recover.

"That's fascinating news, I'm sure, although I have no idea what recurionium is."

"Let me educate you: it's a paralytic agent commonly used as a surgical anesthetic. At places like, say, Benedictine Hospital."

I noticed a faint thread of sweat along her hairline.

"I'm about to join the Benedictine board."

"How much is that going to cost Vince?"

"While you're calculating costs, you may want to consider the price of this little visit."

"Justice rarely comes cheap."

"But wild-eyed theories do. Proof, on the other hand, is sometimes impossible to come up with at any price." Marcus appeared in the doorway. "Marcus, would you show Ms. Petrocelli out?"

"We're not done," I said.

"Oh, but I think we are." She walked toward the living room, then turned and smiled. "Do help yourself to a lobster roll on your way out."

Marcus took my elbow and led me down the hallway, through the kitchen, and out a back door to a small landing. Just as he turned to go back into the house, I played him his message to Esmerelda.

"Either you talk to me, or to the police."

He cocked his head.

"Name your price."

"The truth."

"I had some business dealings with Esmerelda."

"What kind of business dealings?"

"Daphne had certain needs. I made sure they were met."

"So you paid for her heroin? And when she was hooked, you laced that heroin with poison and then strung her up from the rafters to make it look like suicide?"

He turned and walked back into the house.

But not before I noticed a smudge of lipstick on his left ear.

FORTY-NINE

"Unfortunately the evidence is all circumstantial," Chevrona said to me on my cell as I drove home.

"Haven't killers been convicted on circumstantial evidence?"

"They have, but it's tough. And Daphne's body has been cremated, which means it's impossible to prove that she was exposed to the recurionium. And even if Marcella was paying for Daphne's heroin, that doesn't make her guilty of murder. Add to all that the fact the death was ruled a suicide and the DA over in Dutchess is very disinclined to pursue the case, and you have a deck that is seriously stacked against us."

"Are you saying it's all over?"

"I'm saying we need some hard evidence."

I made a U-turn and headed back down to the lighthouse parking lot.

FIFTY

I FOUND MAD JOHN sitting on the riverbank, fishing. He looked subdued, almost pensive.

"Can you take me back down to Esmerelda's tonight?" I asked.

He gave me a sad smile and nodded.

I went to the hardware store and bought two metal saws and a fresh supply of flashlight batteries. If there was recurionium in that drawer in Esmerelda's kitchen, it might have Marcus's fingerprints on it. And if I got really lucky, Marcella's. Maybe it could be traced back to its supplier and proven to have come from the surgical cart at Benedictine.

At a little after eight, just as darkness descended, I grabbed the saws and two flashlights and headed down to the river.

Mad John wasn't at home. I looked around at his scavenged bounty. Something in the pile of electronics, dead computers, and old cameras caught my eye—just as I was trying to make the connection, Mad John appeared through the reeds, stealthy and silent, like an Indian guide. He was still in a strange mood. His eyes were darting around and he kept tugging at his beard.

"How's it going?" I asked.

He just gave a miserable shrug.

We headed down to his inlet, climbed on board the raft, and he pushed off. It was a clear dry night, cooler, moonless and very dark. I was keyed-up, fighting down my anxiety, but I was way past the halfway point in this tunnel and backing out butt-first was out of the question. I needed answers.

"No singing tonight?" I asked Mad John.

"Bad night," he said, looking out at the river.

As we made our way down river, the red running lights of the boats looked like warning lights. The river was still and smooth as glass, black glass. As I looked out over the water, it came to me— what I'd noticed in the pile of detritus back at Mad John's was an old Polaroid camera. I thought of the photographs of Daphne that I'd discovered under her mattress, the lost desperate lust. Taken with an old Polaroid. Then it came back to me—that faint swampy smell in Daphne's bedroom.

"Mad John, are you sure you didn't know Daphne Livingston?"

He looked at me from across the raft, his eyes shining in the darkness. Then he turned back to his rowing.

We were silent for a little while, then I said, "She was an amazing woman, wasn't she?"

The oar moved steadily through the water, then I heard his barely audible voice. "I loved Daphne."

"Did you?"

"I loved her so much."

"Tell me," I said.

"One day last summer I was across the river on my raft, just, you know, noodling around, and there was this woman up in the gazebo and she waved at me and I waved back, and then she walked down the grass and came over the railroad tracks and she said 'hello' and laughed, and her laugh was life itself and she offered me a glass of wine..." He just kept rowing but I could hear him crying. "She was so kind to me, she *knew* me, who I really really was, and she loved me for that...oh, and she was wild, wicked and wild, my baby-lady, we had fun times...me and my baby-lady."

Mad John started to moan, a low breathy keening. Then he put down his oar and curled into a fetal position. "I did a bad bad thing."

"What bad thing did you do, Mad John?"

"She met the witch and the witch got her hooked and kept her fed, fed with death."

"...and so you killed the witch."

The raft was starting to drift out into the middle of the river.

"Daphne was my baby-lady," he wept.

We floated down the black river in the black night and I felt hollowed out, numb. The world was quiet and there was only grief.

We both heard it a split-second before we saw it: the boat that tore out of the night and rammed into the raft, splitting it in two, sending us flying into the water. The wind was knocked out of me. I swallowed river water, sputtered, and struggled to stay afloat. Then Mad John was next to me, holding me up.

"Take off your clothes," he ordered, "or they'll take you down."

I reached underwater and frantically pulled off my sneakers. My jeans felt like a layer of lead. I peeled them off as Mad John buoyed me. Suddenly I was lighter, could kick and keep my head above water.

"They're coming back!" he said. "Stay low!"

We watched with alligator eyes as the boat came closer. It was a speedboat and I made out the outline of a single figure at the wheel ... a man ... Marcus. He killed the engine and as the boat glided *closer* he leaned over the edge, scanning the water. Something glinted in his hand—a gun.

Mad John disappeared underwater. It grew calm for a moment and then he shot up out of the water and grabbed the gun from Marcus's hand. Then he disappeared.

"Fuck!" Marcus cursed.

Marcus picked up a crowbar and scanned the water. He spotted me and turned the wheel in my direction. Mad John vaulted himself up and over on the other side of the boat, screaming, "WHAAAA!" He tackled Marcus. I swam over and clambered onboard. They were rolling around on deck and I grabbed the crowbar and yanked it out of Marcus's hand, threw it overboard. They were up on their knees now, Marcus was twice Mad John's size and he got a grip on him, picked him up, and tossed him overboard. Then he turned to me.

I was ready. Before he could stand up I kneed him under the jaw and his head flew back. Then I kicked him in the chest, then the stomach. He was stunned. I grabbed a flashlight and brought it down on his skull.

Knocked the motherfucker out cold.

FIFTY-ONE

"I want the truth, the whole story," I said to Marcus. He wasn't in much of a position to argue, what with him being down on the ground with his hands tied behind his back. We were in a small swampy clearing near Mad John's moorings.

"The whole story!" Mad John cackled, jumping up and down.

"Fuck you," Marcus said.

"I'm cold and wet and pissed," I said, kneeling down and looking him in the eye.

He spit in my face.

"Now that was uncalled for," I said. "You're just lucky I'm a pacifist. Mad John, you have a bucket handy?"

Mad John gave a leap of assent and then disappeared into the reeds.

"I'm figuring Vince and Marcella have set you up nice and clean to be their fall guy. Hey, you want to end up in prison while they party, that's your business."

Mad John reappeared with a big plastic bucket.

"Fill it with river water, and make sure you get some muck in there," I said.

Mad John dunked the bucket into the Hudson and carried it over.

"Tip it on big boy here," I said.

Mad John tipped the bucket over Marcus's head, coating him with mud and slime. He winced and sputtered and writhed.

"I think one more bucket will do it. See if you can find any snakes." I knew from my practice that a lot of men had a primal terror of snakes—it was a whole phallic thing.

Mad John crouched down on the bank and scooped up a bucket that was more muck than water, sifting through it with his hands. "I got one! I got one!" he said, proudly holding up a long wriggling snake.

Marcus's eyes went wide with fear. "Keep that fucking snake away from me!"

"Then talk."

He didn't.

"Why don't you introduce them?" I said.

Mad John held the snake close to Marcus's face—it writhed in the air and brushed his cheek.

"*Okay, I'll talk!! Just get that thing away from me!!*"

Mad John pulled back. Marcus took a deep breath, exhaled, and his face slackened in resignation.

"First rule of my job: don't touch the boss's booty. I'm such a fuckup," he said bitterly. "Bitch started parading that body around in front of me."

"So you started screwing Marcella," I said. "Then what?"

"She's talking to me about her big plans, to become a celebrity and all that. Says she'll always take care of me. So she sends me out to make nice with Esmerelda. Man, was she a freak."

"Then Marcella booted the poison at Benedictine Hospital, and Esmerelda put it in Daphne's heroin," I said.

"Marcella paid her fifty grand. Well, she paid her half and then when Daphne was dead she didn't want to pay the second half."

"And so the piper sang…" I said.

"Yeah, whatever, will you untie me please," Marcus pleaded.

"Not so fast," I said. "So you waited in the woods until Daphne shot up the bad heroin, then you ran into the summerhouse and strung up her body."

Marcus nodded miserably.

"What about Vince Hammer?" I asked.

"Far as I know, that slick bastard is clean. This was all Marcella. The conniving bitch. But listen, I didn't *kill* that old hag. She was already dead."

"I think you're what's known as an accessory to the murder."

There was a pause and Marcus suddenly looked like a very sad little boy.

"I'm royally fucked, aren't I?"

"Yeah, I think you are."

"I just found a new friend," Mad John said, as the snake slithered around his neck.

FIFTY-TWO

I WAS SITTING IN Detective Chevrona Williams's office at the State Police barracks, wrapped in a blanket. Chevrona walked in, handed me a cup of undrinkable coffee, and said, "Not smart."

I tried to look contrite.

"But effective," she said. "Marcus Randall just signed a full confession. Marcella Sedgwick is also in custody. She's not talking, has hired a big-shot lawyer, and will be out on bail in about half an hour."

"What about Vince Hammer?"

"It looks like he's clean, completely clean," Chevrona said. "This was Marcella's baby, her ticket to Hammer, the estate, and who knows what from there."

"The statehouse, the White House, the history books, I think she's one of those women whose ambition is beyond measure. She's pretty fascinating—Lady MacBeth in a yogatard," I said. "Thanks to Josie, I found out that Marcella grew up in a shack in rural Tennessee—her real name is Amber Lundy. She's brilliant, all her degrees are real, she could have made a name for herself without resorting to murder, but whatever it is that's driving her got the best of her."

"What would you guess that is?"

"I'd have to get her on the couch to know with any certainty, but I'd say the key here may be a profound narcissism. Kids who grow up in desperate situations learn at an early age to find their solace and strength in themselves, they retreat from the pain around them and create their own self-centered world. It's a survival mechanism, and a healthy one up to a point—Marcella went way past that point. Add to that a deep shame at her background, and rage and envy and craving of privilege. Then there's her beauty and sex appeal—this is a woman who has been turning men's heads her entire life. This sexual power and confidence is very real and very heady. It took her a lot further than her degrees. But it also may have led to her grandiosity and hubris, which in turn led to her fatal mistake."

"Not paying Esmerelda the second half of her killing fee?"

"Yes."

"She wanted to be the Queen of the World. Now she's going to be the Queen of Cellblock Sixteen. But I still want a few answers from you. What the hell were you and that lunatic up to out on the river?"

"I was determined to find out who killed Daphne. You might say it turned into an obsession."

"You, of all people, should know that obsessions can be very unhealthy. And breaking and entering is illegal."

"We never actually broke and entered. How is Mad John doing?"

"He's on his second dozen donuts, and he keeps asking how *you're* doing. He seems really concerned."

"Tell him I'm okay."

"You can tell him yourself, we're going to release you both as soon as we finish taking your statements." Chevrona eyeballed me in her Clint Eastwood way. "Why do I have the feeling that you're holding out on me?"

"Maybe because I'm wet and hungry and in shock."

"You figured out who killed Daphne. Any luck with Esmerelda?"

"I haven't been trying to figure out who killed Esmerelda."

"That doesn't answer my question."

I took a sip of coffee. "Could I get a donut?"

Chevrona got up. "Frosted?"

"Pink, please," I said, crossing my legs.

While she went to get the donut, I tried to figure out what to do. Mad John had brutally murdered a human being. Not good. But Esmerelda was a heartless drug dealer who had helped ruin the lives of hundreds of kids. She'd let heroin she knew was tainted hit the streets. And she had been a paid accomplice in Daphne's murder.

What good would turning in Mad John accomplish? He would probably get off by reason of insanity, or do his time in a mental hospital. Except for a fit of passion and a chainsaw, he was an upstanding little guy. He loved the river and was fighting to protect it. He may well have saved my life out there. Sure he was insane, but who's perfect? He was a lot saner than, say, Glenn Beck. And I cared about him.

Chevrona came in and handed me a pink-frosted donut. She sat back down and eyed me.

"So … what *have* you found out about Esmerelda's murder?"

"You're the one who told me to keep my nose out of all this."

"Your evasions are only increasing my suspicion that you're holding out on me."

I took a bite of donut and composed my response. "I can say in all honesty that I have no theories on who killed Esmerelda."

Just facts.

Chevrona gave me a skeptical look.

"Now can you please tell me how *you're* doing?" I asked.

FIFTY-THREE

"Could I have the turkey shepherd's pie, please," I said to Pearl.

"Make that two," Zack added quickly.

Pearl looked at us like we'd just asked for a whole roasted human—but then shock was her perpetual expression. Maybe she was just more in touch with her feelings than the rest of us—I mean, does anyone ever really get over the shock of being born? Pearl eventually raised her pencil to her pad and began to write.

"I really wanted the salmon but I knew it would be another twenty minutes," Zack said.

Since Abba was visible in the kitchen we could have just called out our order and saved a lot of time and aggravation, but Abba refused to fire Pearl, praising her "energy." That was Abba—you can take the girl out of Tibet, but you can't take Tibet out of the girl.

When Pearl had shambled off, Zack poured us both glasses of wine. I'd been out at his cabin all afternoon jumping his bones, and we were both in that beyond-mellow place. He leaned across the table and kissed me. "I'm so proud of you, babycakes." He raised his glass and we toasted. "But next time, mind your own business."

"Don't worry about that, I am *never* getting involved in anyone else's *mishigas* again," I said, taking a sip of my wine. "Never."

George walked into Chow, looking despondent.

"Hey, Georgie-boy, wanna join us for dinner?" Zack asked.

"Eat? How could I possibly eat, my life is over." Then he started quivering and his eyes filled with tears. "Dwayne left me."

"It's my treat," Zack said.

George shuffled over and sat down with a sigh. "I'd kill myself but I'm already dead," he said, taking a roll and slathering it with butter.

"What happened?"

"The world hates beauty and happiness. It wants to crush them into a bitter powder of loneliness and regret," George said as a tear rolled down his cheek, and he picked up my wineglass and took a deep swallow. "His wife found out, *that's* what happened." Then his face dissolved into a mass of tears as he finished my wine and poured himself another glass.

Zack put a hand on his shoulder. "Oh, come on, buddy. You'll be okay; we still love you."

George shuddered   "Don't touch me, please. I never want to be touched again. It only leads to heartbreak and agony."

"I don't want to fuck you, dude, I just want to cheer you up," Zack said.

"Cheer me up? Cheer me up?" George said, reaching for another roll. "If you want to cheer me up, kill me and put me out of my misery."

"George, have you seen that guy who just moved in over the Laundromat?" I said.

"Janet, you really are a walking faux pas, the MVP in the World Series of Insensitivity. You have less depth than a plastic wading pool and less empathy than a concrete block. The love of my life has just dumped me and you want me to start thinking about *another* man. There will *never ever ever* be another man in my life." This triggered a fresh flood of tears, followed by a full glass of wine, followed by a disinterested shrug, and then, "I didn't know anyone had moved in over the Laundromat."

"The gang's all here," Abba said, bringing a plate of tuna tartare over to the table.

"*I'm* not here," George said. "I'm dead."

"So is River Landing," Abba said, sitting down and helping herself to Zack's wine. "Apparently Vince Hammer is so shook up that he's withdrawing his proposal. He may come back in a few years when all the publicity has died down, but the project is permanently tainted and the opposition is only growing."

"I will give Janet a petit soupçon of credit," George said. "Speaking of soupçon, Abba, could I have the roasted pepper soup, the endive salad, the free-range braised chicken with all the sides, and a double slice of chocolate cake with ice cream and whipped cream. Oh, and Zack, could you run down the street and get us another bottle of wine, please?"

Zack rolled his eyes but got up and headed down to the liquor store.

The three of us sat there for a short bit.

"Well, Janet, you really made your mark up here," Abba said.

"Yeah, you have, kiddo," added George.

"No big deal," I said. "You know how it is—one thing leads to another."

FIFTY-FOUR

I POKED MY HEAD into Josie's room, Sputnik by my side. She was in bed, reading Stephen King. Two suitcases were on the floor by the door.

"Big day tomorrow," I said.

She nodded.

"I'm sure they're a terrific family."

She nodded again.

"The check came today for the two squeeze toys you sold on eBay. I owe you your commission."

"I only accept cash."

"Thatta girl."

I went over and sat on the edge of her bed, fussed with her blanket.

"I'm proud of you, Josie."

"Thank you for being my friend," she said.

"Thank you for being mine. You were a big help in solving this murder. And, hey, Troy is only about fifty miles away. What do you

229

say I give you a couple of weeks to settle in, then I come up and take you out to dinner?"

She nodded. I touched her cheek. I could see that, like me, she was willing herself to stay cool. She was going to need that strength a lot more than she needed some soapy farewell.

"See you in the morning." I kissed her forehead and stood up. "Come on, Sput."

I went into my bedroom and got undressed. I was exhausted, in that bone-deep way that feels like release. Sputnik curled up on his rug. I crawled under the covers. The moon was almost full and moonlight spread across the ceiling.

Just as I was halfway to dreamland, there was a ping on my window.

I swung my legs over the side of my bed and looked down to my ratty backyard.

There was Mad John, with a pile of debris tucked under his arm, traipsing through town in the moonlight, gathering the makings of his new raft.

He waved.

I hesitated.

Then I waved back.

THE END

ACKNOWLEGMENTS

For their support and guidance, I'm grateful to Terri Bischoff, Brian Farrey, Connie Hill, Steven Pomije, and everyone else at wonderful Midnight Ink.

Special thanks to Sue Ann Jafferian, who is as generous as she is talented and adorable; to David Dolittle, who helped me find Janet; to Alice McCauley, for the words and so much else; to Dr. Kurt Gress, for sharing his expertise; to Brian DeFiore, for being such a pro; to Mameve Medwed, for reading and for just being.

Also to the folks in the Hudson Valley/Catskills, for endless inspiration. Extra special thanks to Louie Ruggiero, for thirty years of friendship and flowers. And to Steve McCauley, for everything.

ABOUT THE AUTHOR

Sebastian's last novel, *The Hour Between* (Alyson, 2009) won the Ferro-Grumley Award and was a National Public Radio Seasons Readings Selection. The ghostwritten *Charm! by Kendell Hart* (Hyperion, 2008) was a New York Times bestseller. *24-Karat Kids,* written with Dr. Judy Goldstein (St. Martins, 2006) was published in seven languages. His first novel, *The Mentor* (Bantam, 1999) was a Book of the Month Selection.

As a playwright, Sebastian was dubbed "the poet laureate of the Lower East Side" by Michael Musto in *The Village Voice*. His plays—which include *Smoking Newports and Eating French Fries, Beverly's Yard Sale,* and *Under the Kerosene Moon*—have been seen at the Public Theater, The Kitchen, and LaMama, among other venues.

Sebastian has worked as a ghostwriter and editor in every genre imaginable, from business to politics to show business to travel.

A native New Yorker, he now lives with novelist Stephen McCauley in Cambridge, Massachusetts and Saugerties, New York.